Adventure House
Presents

DETECTIVE
SHORT STORIES
March 1939

This reprint edition is a facsmile edition. Variations in print
and quality are mostly attributable to the rough woodpulp
original this reprint edition is based on.

ISBN: 1-59798-112-5

New Material
© 2006 Adventure House

Published by Adventure House
914 Laredo Road
Silver Spring, Md 20901
www.adventurehouse.com
sales@adventurehouse.com

10¢

12 STORIES FOR TEN CENTS

DETECTIVE SHORT STORIES

THE BIGGEST DETECTIVE MAGAZINE

A RED CIRCLE MAGAZINE

Vol. 2, No. 2   March, 1939

THIS MAGAZINE CONTAINS NEW STORIES ONLY!
● NO REPRINTS ARE USED! ●

DETECTIVE SHORT STORIES published every other month by Manvis Publications, Inc. Office of publication, 4600 Diversey Avenue, Chicago, Ill. Editorial and executive offices, RKO Bldg., Radio City, New York, N. Y. Entered as second class matter December 16th, 1936, at the Post Office at Chicago, Ill., under Act of March 3rd, 1879. Entire contents copyright, 1939, by Manvis Publications, Inc. Yearly subscription 60 cents.

I WILL SEND MY FIRST LESSON FREE

It Shows How I Train You at Home in Your Spare Time for a

GOOD JOB IN RADIO

J. E. Smith, President
National Radio Institute
Established 1914

The man who has directed the home study training of more men f o r the Radio Industry t h a n any other man in America.

Service Manager for Four Stores

"I was work- i n g in a ga- rage when I enrolled with N. R. I. In a few months I made enough to pay for the course three or four times. I am now Radio service manager for the M——— Furniture Co., for their four stores."— JAMES E. RYAN, 1535 Slade St., Fall River, Mass.

$40 a Month in Spare Time

"I have a very good spare time trade. At times it is more than I can han- dle. I make on an average of $40 per month profit, and that is spare time, working week ends and some eve- nings." — IRA BIVANS, 218½ E. 3rd St., R o c k Falls, Ill.

Earnings Tripled by N. R. I. Training

"I have been doing nicely, thanks to N. R. I. Training. My present earnings a r e about three times what they were be- for I took the Course. I consider N. R. I. Training the finest in the world."— BERNARD COSTA, 201 Kent St., Brooklyn, N. Y.

Clip the coupon and mail it. I will prove I can train you at home in your spare time to be a RADIO EX- PERT. I will send you my first lesson FREE. Ex- amine it, read it, see how clear and easy it is to un- derstand—how practical I make learning Radio at home. Men without Radio or electrical knowledge be- come Radio Experts, earn more money than ever as a result of my Training.

Get Ready Now for Jobs Like These

Radio broadcasting stations employ engineers, operators, station managers and pay up to $5,000 a year. Fixing Radio sets in spare time pays many $200 to $500 a year —full time jobs with Radio jobbers, manufacturers and dealers as much as $30, $50, $75 a week. Many Radio Experts open full or part time Radio sales and repair businesses. Radio manufacturers and jobbers employ testers, inspectors, foremen, engineers, servicemen, and pay up to $6,000 a year. Automobile, police, aviation, commercial Radio, loud speaker systems are newer fields offering good opportunities now and for the fu- ture. Television promises to open many good jobs soon. Men I trained have good jobs in these branches of Radio. Read how they got their jobs. Mail coupon.

Why Many Radio Experts Make $30, $50, $75 a Week

Radio is young—yet it's one of our large industries. More than 28,000,000 homes have one or more Radios. There are more Radios than telephones. Every year mil- lions of Radios get out of date and are replaced. Mil- lions more need new tubes, repairs. Over $50,000,000 are spent every year for Radio repairs alone. Over 5,000,- 000 auto Radios are in use; more are being sold every day, offering more profit-making opportunities for Radio experts. And RADIO IS STILL YOUNG, GROWING, expanding into new fields. The few hundred $30, $50, $75 a week jobs of 20 years ago have grown to thousands. Yes, Radio offers opportunities—now and for the future!

Many Make $5, $10, $15 a Week Extra in Spare Time While Learning

The day you enroll, in addition to our regular Course, I start sending Extra Money Job Sheets; show you how to do Radio repair jobs. Throughout your training I send plans and directions that made good spare time money—$200 to $500—for hundreds, while learning.

How You Get Practical Experience While Learning

I send you special Radio equipment; show you how to conduct experiments, build circuits illustrating impor- tant principles used in modern Radio receivers, broad- cast stations and loud-speaker installations. This 50-50 method of training—with printed instructions and working with Radio parts and circuits—makes learning at home interesting, fascinating, practical. I ALSO GIVE YOU A MODERN, PROFESSIONAL ALL-

WAVE, ALL-PURPOSE RADIO SET SERVICING INSTRUMENT to help you make good money fixing Radios while learning and equip you with a profes- sional instrument for full time jobs after graduation.

Money Back Agreement Protects You

I am so sure I can train you to your satisfaction that I agree in writing to refund every penny you pay me if you are not satisfied with my Lessons and Instruction Service when you finish. A copy of this agreement comes with my Free Book.

Find Out What Radio Offers You

Act Today. Mail the coupon now for sample lesson and 64-page book. They're free to any fellow over 16 years old. They point out Radio's spare time and full time opportunities and those coming in Television; tell about my training in Radio and Television; show you letters from men I trained, telling what they are doing and earning. Find out what Radio offers YOU! MAIL COUPON in an envelope, or paste on a postcard—NOW!

J. E. Smith, President, Dept. 9AK1
National Radio Institute, Washington, D. C.

J. E. SMITH, President, Dept. 9AK1
National Radio Institute, Washington, D. C.

Dear Mr. Smith: Without obligating me, send the sample lesson and your book which tells about the spare time and full time opportunities in Radio and explains your 50-50 method of training men at home in spare time to become Radio Experts. (Please write plainly.)

NAME .... AGE.........

ADDRESS ....

CITY... STATE..................... 2 FR

★ ★ ★ ★ ★ SALES MEAN JOBS—BUY NOW! ★ ★ ★ ★ ★

Now *is the time!*

Business is Searching for **YOU,** if . . . .

R IGHT now, in many lines, there is a search for really *good* men—managers, leaders—men who can take charge of departments, businesses, branch offices, and get things humming.

As always, there are not enough ordinary jobs to go 'round—but rarely before, in the history of American business, has there been so much room at the *top!* And new jobs are being created by the business pick-up in many lines—jobs that pay splendidly and that open the way to lifetime success.

Ordinarily, there would be plenty of men to fill these jobs—men in junior positions who had been studying in spare time. But most men have been letting their training slide during these dark years of depression . . . "What's the use?"—You have heard them say. Perhaps there has been some excuse for sticking to any old kind of a job one could get the past few years—but the door is wide open for the man with ambition and ability *NOW!*

And don't let anyone tell you that "Opportunity Only Knocks Once"—that's one of the most untruthful sayings ever circulated. Opportunities flourish for *every* American every day of his life.

Far more to the point is to be ready—to be *prepared*—to make yourself *interesting* to the big-time employer—and LaSalle offers you a short-cut method of qualifying for opportunity jobs in accounting, law, traffic, executive management, and kindred occupations.

LaSalle Extension is 30 years old—averages over 30,000 enrollments a year—60 American firms each employ 500 or more LaSalle-trained men—surveys show that many LaSalle students attain 40% salary increase after graduation—10% of all C.P.A.'s in the U.S.A. are LaSalle-alumni.

Why not find out what LaSalle has done and is doing for men in *your* position? Send and get the facts; see what LaSalle can do for you, personally!

There's no question about it—business is picking up—jobs are looking for *men*—the time has come for you to *qualify* for prosperity. Mail this coupon today!

Are You a New Science-Fiction Reader? —Then Here's Good News!

If you have yet to read your first science-fiction magazine, if you have yet to experience the thrills of knowing what lies ahead in the world of tomorrow, then get in the swing at once and be one of the first to read science-fiction's newest and most sensational s-f magazine— DYNAMIC SCIENCE STORIES! There is nothing like it on any newsstand—there has never been anything like it in science-fiction. It is science-fiction COME OF AGE! Jaded s-f readers are hailing it as the greatest thing that has ever happened to science-fiction. You will hail it as the most exciting experience you have ever had! Sample the contents here and get your copy from your newsdealer today—remember: this issue will go fast, for seasoned science-fiction readers will nab this first issue as a collector's item (Copies of Volume 1, Number 1 of a new magazine, particularly of a specialized sort such as DYNAMIC, kept in good condition, are very valuable in later years).

DYNAMIC SCIENCE STORIES

15c at any newsstand

A Complete Gripping Novel

The Lord of Tranerica..........
..........by Stanton Coblentz

2 Great Long Science Novelettes

Mutineers of Space...........
.......by Lloyd Arthur Eshbach

Quest of Zipantoric...........
.....by Robert Moore Williams

2 Super-Science Short Stories

The Mercurian Menace........
..............by Nelson S. Bond

The Message from the Void.....
............by Hubert Mavity

Science Departments

The Test Tube ....

Through the Telescope...........

Or are you a seasoned science-fiction reader?
—There's Good News for YOU on Page 10!

IMAGINE THEIR JOY

WHEN THEY FOUND THEY COULD PLAY

This easy as A.B.C. way!

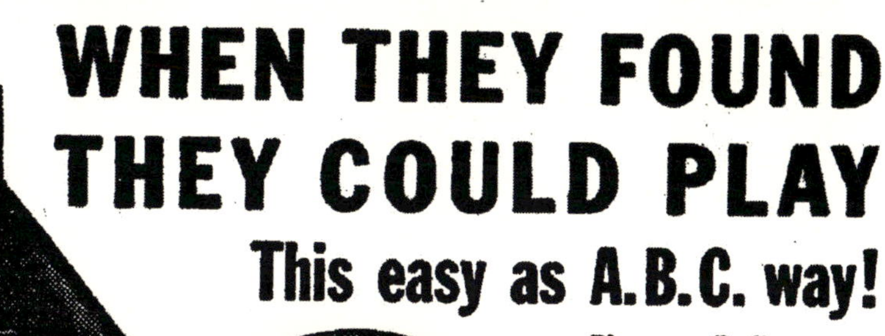

Plays on Radio

I am happy to tell you that for four weeks I have been on the air over our local radio station. So thanks to your institution for such a wonderful course.

*W. H. S., Alabama

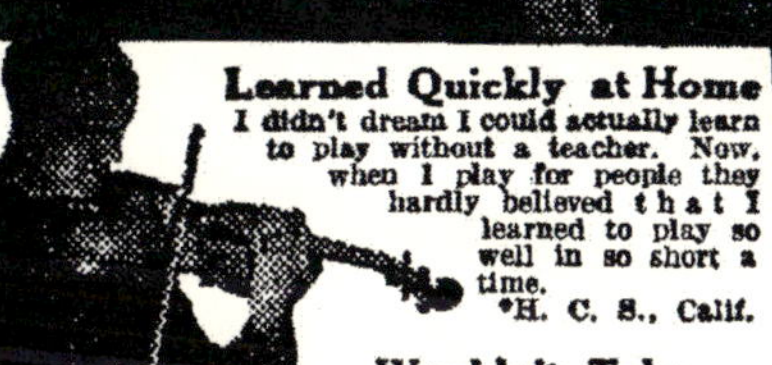

Learned Quickly at Home

I didn't dream I could actually learn to play without a teacher. Now, when I play for people they hardly believed t h a t I learned to play so well in so short a time.
*H. C. S., Calif.

Wouldn't Take $1000 for Course

The lessons are so simple that anyone can understand them. I have learned to play by note in a little more than a month. I wouldn't take a thousand dollars for my course.

*S. E. A., Kansas City, Mo.

Surprised Friends

I want to say that my friends a r e greatly surprised at the different pieces I can already play. I am very happy to have chosen your method of learning.
*B. F., Bronx, N. Y.

Best Method by Far

Enclosed is my last examination sheet for my course in Tenor Banjo. This completes my course. I have taken lessons before under teachers, but my instructions with you were by far the best.
*A. O., Minn.

What Instrument Would You Like To Play?

JUST name your instrument and we'll show you how you can learn to play it—quickly, easily, in spare time at home. Never mind if you don't know one note of music from another—don't worry about "special talent". And forget all you've ever heard about music's being hard to learn.

The truth of the matter is that *thousands now play who never thought they could!* Yes, men and women everywhere have discovered this amazingly easy way to learn music at home. Now they are enjoying the thrilling satisfaction of playing the piano, violin, guitar, saxophone or other favorite instruments. Some of them are playing in orchestras and over the radio; others are teaching music,

making money in spare or full time. And thousands are having the time of their lives playing for their own enjoyment and the entertainment of their friends.

It all came about when they wrote to the U. S. School of Music for the Free Booklet and Demonstration Lesson that show you how EASY it is to learn music at home this modern way. No tedious study and practice, no tiresome exercises. You learn to play *by playing*—start right in almost at once with the melody of a simple tune! It takes only a few minutes a day and the cost is trifling; you save the expense of a private teacher. Does it sound too good to be true? Mail the coupon and get the FREE PROOF! U. S. School of Music, 2461 Brunswick Bldg., N. Y. C., N. Y. (Our forty-first year—Est. 1898.)

SEND FOR FREE
DEMONSTRATION LESSON AND BOOKLET

● You'll open your eyes when you find how quickly and easily you can learn to play your favorite instrument. Don't doubt; don't hesitate. Send for the fascinating illustrated booklet that answers all your questions; let the free demonstration lesson show you how this method actually works. There's no cost, no obligation. Just mail the coupon, NOW. (Instruments supplied when needed, cash or credit.)

* *Actual pupil's names on request. Pictures by professional models.*

U. S. SCHOOL OF MUSIC
2461 Brunswick Bldg., New York City, N. Y.

Without cost or obligation to me, please send me your free illustrated booklet and demonstration lesson. I am interested in the instrument checked below:

Piano	Banjo	Trombone
Violin	Mandolin	Flute
Guitar	Ukulele	Piccolo
Piano Accordion	Cornet	Organ
Plain Accordion	Trumpet	Drums and Traps
Saxophone	Harp	Harmony and Composition
Cello	Clarinet	Voice Culture
Hawaiian Guitar		

Name .... Have you
This Instru.? ....

Address ....

City.. State..................................

Are You a Seasoned Science-Fiction Reader? —Then Here's Good News!

First letters received on the NEW MARVEL SCIENCE STORIES — the science magazine that YOU helped establish and edit—claim it's the finest thing that has ever happened to science-fiction! The third issue, you know (February, now on stands) is the first issue to grow out of the editorial policy that you demanded. Sample the contents here, then get a copy from your newsdealer at once. Remember—this edition is limited, and there will be no back copies that you can pick up later. Nab your copy now while the nabbing is good!

Great Super-Science Novel

After World's End.............
............by Jack Williamson

2 Dynamic Science Novelettes

Faster Than Light...by D. D. Sharp

The Second Moon.............
........by R. R. Winterbotham

2 Exciting Short Stories of Days to Come

The Weather Adjudicator......
..........by Stanton Coblentz

Vast Beyond Concept..........
................by Hal Remson

A Sensational Article

Atlantropa—The Improved Continent.........by Willy Ley

A sensational scientific solution for land-grabbing, war-crazy Europe!

Science Reader's Departments

Or are You a New Science-Fiction Reader?

—THERE'S GOOD NEWS FOR YOU ON PAGE 8!

DEATH A LA CARTE

By ERIC HOWARD

Author of "No Alias For Homicide," etc.

What do you do when you find a pretty girl, gun in hand, standing over a corpse—particularly when that girl has stolen your car—and your heart?

Then Marge came out, and she had been crying

I'M supposed to stick around this drive-in eatery, on the boulevard, and keep my eyes open. That was the idea of Dick Hughes, head of the local office of the agency I'm with. There was a guy variously known as Steve Malone, George Mellon, and Ralph Melbourne—and maybe a lot more monickers—that Dick wanted picked up. Rumor had it that this guy had a moll working in the eatery. We knew the moll and she was easy on the eyes.

Her name, embroidered on the jacket of her uniform, was Marge. She had a tip-winning smile for everybody, and she got to be pretty friendly with me. I drove in every day about one, had

crashed Mrs. Amy Dexter-Smith-Hopkins-Fair's party and got out with the much-married Amy's jewels. On the way out, the mug had half-killed a loyal chauffeur who had tried a flying tackle. The chauffeur might die any day and then Steve Malone would be wanted for murder. We wanted him because Amy's trinkets were heavily insured

something to eat and a bottle of beer, then sat there in my coupe, pretending to go over sales reports. I was supposed to be the crew manager for a bunch of coffee and spice salesmen.

I was kind of sorry that Marge was mixed up with this Malone guy. She was a nice kid, and it was too bad she had got tangled with the boy who

and our agency represented the insurance company. The main idea was to get the stuff back, but if the cops wanted Malone we'd cooperate to the extent of handing him over—if we ever got our hands on him.

I had been covering the eatery detail for a week. Dick Hughes had a kid working the morning shift as bus-boy

13

and another man took on where I left off, in the late afternoon.

I stuffed my alleged reports in a brief case and beckoned to Marge. She came over, smiling. She's a brown-haired twist, with big gray eyes and a wide mouth. She has a way of looking at you with her head on one side. Not too pretty, but there's something about her. She made me feel I could get along with her for quite a while. I had to remind myself that she was tangled with Malone, which wasn't so good.

"Give me a barbecued beef on rye and a cup of java, babe," I said.

"Coming up, Mr. Blake," she said.

AS she went over to the counter, to turn in the order, I saw this other dame come up in a taxi. She got out at the curb, told the driver to wait, and walked into the eatery parking lot. I got a look at her. And was she something? A doll and no mistake. Marge was a good-looking kid, in a simple, wholesome way; but this doll had style and clothes and dough written all over her. She was beautiful to start with; then the beauticians and the hair-dressers and all the rest added to it.

She went into the pay phone booth and called a number. She had quite a wait and she stood there, looking out of the glass door. I took a long look at her and I wouldn't forget her soon. She looked sad or mad, or both. When she finally got her party, she began talking fast, and she was mad. Finally she hung up, stood there undecided for a while, then came out. Marge was bringing my sandwich on a tray. The other dame looked at Marge, then opened her hand-bag and looked into it. Marge fussed around me a while and the doll fidgetted.

When Marge left me, the doll started for the ladies' room and from the door beckoned to Marge. Marge looked surprised, perhaps a little afraid, then followed her. They were in there a few minutes. Then the doll came out, fast, and walked to her taxi. The cab was pulling away when Marge came out. She had been crying and she was wiping her eyes. I tapped the horn button lightly and she came over, trying to choke off the sniffles and give me her usual smile. She couldn't quite make it.

"Why the tears, babe?" I asked. "Tell papa."

"I—I was slicing onions," she said.

"Sure it wasn't bologney? Kid, there comes a time when every gal needs a friend. If you ever do, give me a chance. If anything is bothering you, come and weep on my shoulder."

She grinned up at me. "Thanks. But nothing bothers me. Honest, I was slicing onions."

"Okay," I said.

And she knew that I knew onions didn't bring on those tears.

A little later I pulled out. The man who took on where I left off was parked across the street. Marge worked through the evening rush, until nine. I decided I'd put in a little overtime, tonight, and see what I could find out.

I was back by eight-thirty, and just in time. Marge was hurrying down to the corner, wearing a long coat over her uniform. A big yellow bus was pulling into the curb. She swung aboard and I took off after the bus.

It was a long ride, across town, out another boulevard into a new apartment house district. Marge got off at a corner, crossed the boulevard and walked down a side street. She seemed to be looking for a number. I parked under a tree and followed her on foot. She turned in at a small apartment building.

I stood out there for a while, trying to figure it out. The doll had told her to come here. Marge hadn't wanted to come. But here she was. The Malone guy was probably inside and for some reason he wanted to see Marge. It was nice to think she didn't want to see him. But Malone and the doll had something on her; they had made her come.

Well, here was my chance to grab off Malone. I walked up to the door and shoved it open. I looked at the names on the mail boxes just inside. There were eight apartments in the building, four upstairs and four down. One of the names was Mrs. Mona Melbourne. Her apartment was upstairs, in front. Melbourne was one of the monickers the Malone guy used. But if the doll I had seen was his moll, where did Marge fit in? Maybe he was a bigamist.

I WENT upstairs, moved along the hall towards the Melbourne dame's apartment. I began hearing things right away.

A deep-voiced mug was saying, "Now where is he?"

And Marge was gasping, "I tell you I don't know! Mona said he'd be here. That's why I came. If I had known where he is, why would I come here to see him?"

She got her face slapped, hard, for talking back.

The Mona dame said, "You do know! And you're going to tell us. We're not going to let that rat double-cross us."

"No, you're double-crossing him," Marge handed it back. "He took all the chances, did everything. And all the time you two were cheating, using him. He got wise to you, that's all, in time. He ran out on you, as he should have long ago. You never loved him, Mona; you got him crazy about you and used him—made him do the things your lover hadn't nerve enough to do! Of all the cheap, contemptible little—"

The deep-voiced guy slapped her harder. He must have knocked her off her pins. I heard her go down. I wanted

to bust in and hand him a couple, but I was supposed to be working for the agency, not just out to protect Marge. I had to find out things. So far all I had learned was that Mona was married to the Malone guy, but had another boy friend; Malone, getting wise, had pulled the Amy job and ducked. Now Mona and the boy friend were mad. They wanted to locate Malone. But why did they think he would take Marge into his confidence?

"You're going to talk before you leave here," the mug threatened her. "When I start working you over—"

There was a shot, a scream, the fall of a heavy body. Then the door flew open. I got back against the wall, out of the light. Marge came running out, heading for the stairs. She was thrusting a gun into her handbag.

I could have stopped her, I guess. But I wanted to see what had happened inside.

"Stop her!" the other dame was yelling. "Police! She killed—"

She shut up when I walked in.

A big man, wearing a loud checked suit, was on the floor as dead as he would ever be. A slug had completely destroyed his heart action and two fifty cent cigars in his vest pocket. I gave him a second look and recognized him. Samuel Barron, The Credit Jeweler, who ran a big store on Broadway and advertised his jewelry bargains in the papers. Wedding rings, no money down, were his big special. I had heard something about how his collectors hounded the guys who bought engagement and wedding rings, or trinkets for their babes, once they had been hooked.

"What happened, lady?" I said.

Mona was staring down at her Sammy, as though she couldn't believe it.

"There was a gun on the sofa," she said. "I had forgotten it. She sat down there—and then, all at once, she picked up the gun and fired. He fell and— You must have seen her! Why didn't you stop her?"

"Me stop a dame with a gat?" I laughed. "Not me. She shot this guy without provocation?"

"Yes! Shot him down in cold blood! It's murder!"

"Well, well," I said. "Didn't I hear him pushing her around? Didn't he hand her a few smacks? Didn't he tell her what he was going to do to her? He was a mutt to talk like that when this gat was right by her hand. I'll call the cops."

The phone was on a little table, at the end of the sofa. Right back of the sofa, there was an open casement window. It had a built-in screen, the kind you can pull up and down, and there was a hole in the screen—a neat little hole, caused by the passing of a bullet.

I went to the window, looked out. Ten feet away was another apartment house. The windows were on a level with this one, but on the second floor they were all dark.

A SHIVER ran up my spine. There was somebody over there who liked to shoot people. I thought he might like me for a target. I jerked on the Venetian blinds and they clattered down.

"Nuts," I said to the doll. "The twist that ran out of here didn't bump your boy friend. The slug that got him came from over there."

Her eyes went wild and her mouth was open. "She had the gun in her hand," she said. "Then there was a shot and—"

"Sure, but she didn't pull the trigger." I picked up the phone, called headquarters and asked for Mike Reardon, homicide man. "Come and get it, Mike, my fran. The big ice and gold man, Sam Barron, has been bumped. His girl friend is here and thinks she

eye-witnessed it. Yeah, I'll wait till you get here. Sure, I'll hold her. She's a beaut."

The doll was looking at me, her mouth twisting.

"You won't keep me here!" she said and made a dive for a table drawer.

I caught her before she got it open and pulled her away. She was still beautiful, but she looked mad enough to bite. I decided she wasn't my type. I pushed her over on the sofa and sat down in front of her.

"Play nice," I said. "If you've got any more guns stowed away around this arsenal, don't grab 'em. I might have to break your jawbone before you shot and I'd hate to bust up anything so pretty. Tell me things. You might need a pal. Who was the frail that was here? What did you want her to tell you?"

She clammed on me, wouldn't say a thing.

"Then I'll tell you, sister," I said. "You were married—maybe you're still married—to a guy sometimes known as Steve Malone. Steve was useful in his way, but you've been playing around with Sammy Barron, the ice man. Steve got hep and ran out on you, after pulling a nice job. You and Sammy wanted your split, because you planned the job. Steve was just the guy with the guts to pull it off. But he took a powder and kept the haul. Maybe he found a better fence than Sammy. You wanted him, so you got that girl to come here and—"

"She killed Sam!" the doll spat fire. "That's an old hole in the screen. It was there when I moved in. She killed him and I hope they hang her!"

"It took you a long time to think that up," I said. "And it won't help. The technical boys can tell just when the bullet came through the screen, what calibre it was and so on. My guess is that Steve Malone popped off at Sammy. Now what is that girl to Steve?"

The doll's face went hard. "I don't know what you're talking about," she said.

Mike Reardon, big and red-faced and with his hat on one side, filled the door. He looked us over for a minute, then walked in. Three other guys from headquarters came in with their tools.

I gave Mike the dope I had. He went to the window, looked at the screen, grunted, then sent a man over next door. I waited beside Mike until the dick showed up in there, in the apartment directly opposite.

"It's empty, Mike," he called, leaning out of the window. "It's been vacant for a week."

Mike grunted again. "Look around in there. See if you can find anything."

THE dick found a few shreds of cigar tobacco on the floor below the window and some cigar ash on the sill.

"Okay," Mike said. "We'll put it through the lab. Maybe we'll learn something."

"I'll leave you to chin with the lady," I said.

"Wait a minute, Blake," Mike looked at me, his blue eyes narrowed down. "How come you were here? Huh? You know the girl that ran out?"

"Yeah, I know her," I said. "Maybe I can find her. I'll tell you, Mike. I saw this dame throw a scare into her. When she started out for this place, I tailed her. I kind of like the kid. I thought maybe she was in a jam and—"

"Romantic, huh?" Mike said. "Like hell. But you guys can't tell the truth, unless it's sweated out of you."

"Why, Michael!" I protested.

"Scram!" he said. "We're busy."

I went out, started walking towards my coupe. But it wasn't there. It was gone. Somebody had stolen my car. Dick Hughes wasn't going to like that.

It belonged to the agency. I growled some bad words, automatically, and walked down to the boulevard. If my guess was right, Steve Malone had been in the vacant apartment, waiting for a chance at Sammy and Mona. It was Steve, I'd bet, who had got away with my bus.

I didn't want to tell Mike my wagon had been rolled away. He'd laugh; anyway, he was only interested in homicide. But I ran into a cop at the boulevard corner. I asked him questions.

"Yeah," he said. "A girl went by here in a coop like that, a little while ago. I noticed her on account she clashed the gears somethin' terrible right over there."

"They never learn, do they?" I said, and flagged a cab.

So Marge had copped my car! But I was still betting she had Steve Malone in it, probably in the luggage compartment.

There was nothing for me to do but try to find Marge. I went back to the drive-in beanery, not expecting to find her, but hoping to get a line on her. Where did she live? Not that she'd be home, now that she was running around with the Malone guy.

I felt kind of sad. She was too good a kid to be mixed up with crooks. And it looked like Malone had tossed her out when he fell for the Mona doll. But Marge was still for him a hundred per cent. Dames are like that—especially when the guy in the case is a rat. Or so it seems.

My sidekick from the agency, who wasn't supposed to know me, was still around. He gave me the high-sign. I went up to the beanery counter and grabbed a stool. The manager saw me and I fingered him.

I asked about Marge.

"She quit," he said, mournfully. "I'm sorry to lose her. She's a good kid, a worker, and popular with the customers.

She got off early tonight—told me she had to see a sick relative—and a little while ago she phoned to say she was quitting. She's going to nurse this relative."

"Where does she live?"

"Won't do you no good to chase her," he said. "She's a good kid."

"Nuts," I said. "Where does she live?"

He gave me her address. "Every time I get some good girls like Marge, they get spliced or quit on me. It's a hell of a business. Say, she won't be staying there no more. She said she was going with this relative."

"Man or woman?"

"I didn't ask. Listen, Mister, if you see her, sell her the idea of coming back."

"Sure," I grinned, "unless I marry her myself and take her out of circulation."

I WROTE down Marge's address. I also scribbled a note to the side-kick, telling him she'd quit and I was looking for her and to grab her if she came back. Not that I thought she would come back, but you can never tell; maybe she forgot her favorite lipstick. I passed him the note as I went towards the cab.

Marge lived in a rooming house not far away. The blowsy old dame who ran it liked the kid and was sorry she had moved. She had packed up her stuff and had gone away, driving away —in a friend's car, she said. She had given the old dame the same line about a sick relative.

"Man or woman?" I asked her, too.

"She didn't say. But I know she has an aunt, so mebbe—"

"Where does the aunt live?"

"I don't know."

That helped a lot. Finding Marge wasn't going to be easy. I phoned the agency from a corner drug-store and the guy on night duty at the desk handed me a laugh.

"You've been took," he said. "Some dame grabbed your car."

"Are you telling me? How did you know?"

"She phoned in a while ago, said to tell you she was sorry but she had to borrow it and you'd find the wreck parked on Central between Ninth and Tenth. How's walking, pal?"

"Did you trace her call?" I yelled.

"No. Why should I? I thought it was just one of your dames. Hustle down there and look for the jaloppy. If she was telling the truth, you'll find it. I think it's all a practical joke."

"Why don't Dick hire a guy with brains for your job?"

"I don't know the answer," the mutt said. "But no dame ever rolled away in my buggy—unless I was with her."

I hung up, growling. My taxi driver, in an amiable mood induced by the sweet music of his meter, took me down to Central. I found my wagon, right where Marge said she had left it. I found my key in the switch, where, like a sap, I leave it most of the time. And my flashlight was back of the seat, where I keep it. I took it and raised the luggage compartment door. I played the flash over it.

The dust was all wiped away, by some guy who had been curled up in there. Steve Malone! I was doing all right with my guessing, but that didn't help locate Marge and Steve.

I stuck around there for a long time. It was a neighborhood of cheap apartments and hotels. Steve and Marge were probably hiding out in one of them. But I couldn't crash into every room in every building on the street or within a radius of a few blocks.

Finally I slipped into gear and rolled homeward.

I didn't go to the office the next day and I hung up on Dick Hughes, the boss, when he started telling me what I should have done and what he would have done. I had heard that routine before.

The morning papers played up Sammy Barron's murder. His partner, Henry Morgan, had offered a five grand reward for arrest and conviction. Morgan had his picture in the paper and a statement. He said Barron had been trying to contact jewel thieves who had robbed their store, in the hope of regaining the loot. They had not notified the police because Barron hadn't wanted publicity and had been sure he could make a deal with the thieves. This, according to Morgan, explained what Barron, a married man and a papa, had been doing in the dame's apartment. The natural response to that was, Oh, Yeah?

MONA was being guarded by the police and the D. A., lest the murderer attempt to rub her out. That's all they said about Mona; not a word about her being hitched to Steve Malone. And the cops were also looking for the girl, unnamed, who had taken a powder. That was Marge.

I rolled my wagon out and went down to Central again. I parked some distance from where I had found the car, behind a big truck, and waited. Most of this job is waiting for something to turn up, waiting in the right place. I thought maybe I had picked it.

Before noon I knew I had. Marge came out of one of the hotels. She looked up and down the street. She was frightened. She didn't want to be seen. But she had to go out for something.

I started to get out of the car to follow her, when she turned into an apartment house. Even from where I sat I could see the brass sign: Philip Harris, M. D., Physician and Surgeon. And not much good at it, or he wouldn't be practicing down here.

So Marge needed a sawbones for her sick relative.

She came out with the doc after fifteen minutes. He was a tall, old boy, with alcoholic dignity, and she was tugging at his hand, trying to hurry him. They went into the hotel and I wasn't far behind—close enough, in fact, to see what room they entered.

I was standing by the door a moment later.

And a guy in there with a hoarse voice was saying, "Never mind where I got it, Doc. Just fix it up an' don't talk. That's all you got to do."

I eased my gun around, put my hand on the knob, shoved the door open.

"Okay, Steve," I said. "I want you for the Amy So-and-So jewel job. The cops want you for what you did to Amy's chauffeur, and for killing Sam Barron last night. Take it easy, boy."

Marge was staring at me, speechless, bue she got her breath and burst out, "Mr. Blake! O, please, Mr. Blake! He didn't kill that man!"

"You know this shamus, Marge?" Steve asked.

"Y-yes," she said. "He used to come to the place to eat. I—I didn't know he was a detective until I found his car, last night. I thought he was a real coffee salesman!"

"Uh-huh," Steve said in a flat voce. "And all the time he was waitin' for you to get in touch with me, so he could pick me up." He looked up at me and his face twisted. "Can you wait, cop, till this doc fixes my side?"

"Sure," I said. "Go ahead, Doc. What's wrong with your side, Steve?"

"That was no chauffeur they want me for shootin'. He was a cop, like you, hired to guard the jewels Mrs. Amy D-S-H-F had collected from her various husbands. I didn't want to hurt him—I was givin' him a break, see?— till he shot me. I been goin' around with the slug in me and I think it's poisonin' me now. I got a busted rib, too."

"Where's the swag?"

He smiled with the side of his mouth. "If I take a rap, nobody ever finds it," he said, "and if anybody finds it, I don't take a rap. How's 'at?"

"No use holding out, Steve," I said. "You'll need dough to hire a mouthpiece. Maybe a good one could make it manslaughter instead of first-degree murder. See? On account of Mona. Play ball with me and the insurance company, kick in with the swag, and maybe we'll get you a mouthpiece. We can make a deal. The cops want you for murder."

"For killin' Barron? Nuts! I wasn't around there last night."

"Now, now, Steve," I shook my finger at him.

"He wasn't!" Marge protested. "He was *not*, Mr. Blake! He was no place near that apartment! I know it! He couldn't have done it."

I LOOKED at her. Her face was full of pleading. The way a nice kid will stick to a crook, even a killer, beats all.

"So you say," I observed. "The cops think different. And just where did you meet Steve, then, last night, if not outside the apartment, right after he shot Barron? You swore up and down to Barron you didn't know where he was."

Marge choked back a sob, then whispered: "I didn't then. I ran out of there after—after he was killed. I hardly knew what had happened, because you see I had a gun in my hand and I was going to tell him I'd kill him if he'd slapped me any more. And then he was shot. I—L thought I'd done it, for a minute. But when I got my wits back, I saw the gun was fully loaded. So I knew I hadn't. But I knew Mona would lie—say I had shot Barron. I just had to find Steve!

"Well, I borrowed your car, Mr. Blake. I recognized it and thought it was funny you'd be there, until I saw on the ownership license on the dash that it was an Acme Detective Agency car. Then I knew you'd been watching me, not just coming there to eat or — I had to get to Steve. And it wasn't easy, because I had to find someone who knew where he was and would tell me. Finally," she gulped, "I did. Poor Steve was in a terrible place, hiding, and I brought him here. And now you've found us—and it's all my fault!"

She started to cry, but Steve cut her off with his hard, tough voice. "Okay, Sis, okay! We can take it. Don't cry in front of a cop—it makes 'em feel big."

"Is this guy your brother?" I asked Marge.

"Of course!" she said, as though I should have known. "And now you've arrested him! But he didn't kill that man! He couldn't. He was miles away. He was sick—too sick to move! Oh, please, don't say he killed him!"

"The cops are saying it," I said. "Then there's the chauffeur. If he dies—"

"He won't. He's a cop," Steve snarled. "How about it, Doc?"

The alcoholic doc smiled vaguely. "Be all right. Be all right," he said. "I'll—I'll run along now."

"You screwball!" I said. "It won't be all right! That's blood poisoning. The guy has to go to a hospital. What did you put on there?"

"Just an anti—antiseptic dressing," the doc spluttered.

"You dope, he'll die!" I told him.

Marge screamed.

"Shut up," Steve said. "The cop is tryin' to scare somebody. It's old stuff."

"Listen, Steve," I said, "I'm giving it to you straight. This doc is so pickled he wouldn't know a corn from a cancer. You've got to get to a hospital."

"Sir," the doc said, "I am a member of the medical—"

"But not in good standing," I shut him up. "Marge, if you want this brother of yours to live, run down and phone for an ambulance. And don't run out on me! You're going to need a pal. It could be me."

Marge moved towards the door.

"Don't, Sis!" Steve said. "Don't go!"

"Stevie, I've got to!" she said. "Oh, I've got to!"

AND ran out, sobbing. Steve glared at me, started to cuss.

"I'm saving your life, you punk," I told him. "Show a little gratitude. Why did you drag Marge into this?"

"I didn't," he said. "And if you do, I'll get you, blood poison or no blood poison. She's a good kid."

"Sure," I agreed. "I know that. Tell me things, punk. Who shot Barron if you didn't?"

"Go to hell," he said. Beads of perspiration stood out on his face; he was in pain.

Marge came back, looking frightened, and the ambulance came up to the hotel. They took Steve out. Marge and I went along in my car. The Doc drifted out.

Marge didn't say anything on the way, and I let her cry it out. As we pulled into the hospital parking lot, though, she began to talk.

"Steve was all right till he fell for Mona," she said. "Oh, maybe he was tough, but he wasn't crooked. He never did anything wrong. Mona got him to do things. She got him into this. She planned it all with that man Barron. They needed Steve to—to stick up that party."

"Sure," I said. "I get it. Barron and Mona were like that. Barron was a fence. Mona got Steve to pull the job. Barron was going to take over the junk and pay Steve off. But Steve got wise, Mona was two-timing him with Barron. He knew they were making him the goat. He knew they'd gyp him, let him take the rap if anything happened. So he beat them to it. I get it. But he's in a spot. If that chauffeur dies, and if they try to pin Barron's death on him, it will be bad. But even if they don't, he'll take a rap for the stick-up."

Marge was crying.

"I'm sorry, kid," I told her. "Let's go in and see what the docs say."

I left her talking to a doc, who was not optimistic, and phoned Dick Hughes. He said he'd be right up. He thought he could talk Steve into telling us where the swag was. I didn't think so. Steve was tough enough to hold out.

Marge and I waited there, while the docs went to work on Steve. Dick Hughes came in and gave me a dirty look. I didn't want Marge to hear all the things he'd call me, so I pulled him aside. I made him listen to what I had to say.

I insisted that Marge wasn't in it, in any way, and he couldn't drag her in. I told him Steve couldn't have shot Barron.

"I don't care who shot him," Dick growled. "I want to know where this guy cached Amy's baubles. And I'm going to find out. I'm going in there and make him talk."

He was wrong. The nurse wouldn't let him in. It would be at least two hours before he could see Steve; and, she said gravely, Steve might not live.

Dick swore. He told me I should have worked Steve over before bringing him to the hospital.

"What do you take me for—a cannibal?" I asked him. "The guy might 'a' died on me."

"Who cares — if you learned anything? Who are you working for—me, this crook, or the girl?"

"Listen," I said. "A man has been killed. If we knew who killed Barron—"

"I don't care about that," he growled. "I'm not working for Barron. Let the cops worry. This guy Steve killed him. Why do you think he didn't? Because the twist says so. Don't be a sap! All I want to know is—where did he stow Amy's junk?"

"If he lives, maybe he'll tell you," I said.

I WENT back to Marge. Dick started walking up and down. Big Mike Reardon pushed through the door. He had got the report from the hospital that Steve Malone had been brought here.

"You guys cooperate a lot, don't you?" he snarled. "I want Malone for killing Barron."

Marge gasped and I put my hand over hers.

"He couldn't have done that, Mike," I said. "He wasn't near there."

"Says you!" Mike walked over and stood in front of us. "You're Malone's sister? What kind of cigars does he smoke?"

"Why he never smokes cigars!" Marge said. "Just cigarettes."

"That's what you say. Well, he's taken up cigar smoking lately—expensive cigars, too."

"No," Marge said, shaking her head.

"Yes," said Mike.

"What brand?" I asked.

Mike named it. I got up, grinning.

"Stay here, Marge," I said. "They'll let you in to see Steve as soon as they can. These gentlemen will keep you company. But if they ask a lot of questions, don't answer 'em."

"Where do you think you're going?" Mike wanted to know.

"Yeah," said Dick.

"I want to see a man," I said.

"You're staying here," Mike told me. "Right here."

"Yes, sir," I said meekly, and sat down.

Mike went over to talk to Dick. They were standing near the main door. There was another at the end of the hall. I got up and sprinted for it. Mike yelled, but I was outside and in the jaloppy before he got out.

Barron's vest pocket had been full of the same brand of cigars that Mike said his killer smoked. A lot of people smoked them, but it wouldn't do any harm to check on one.

I went down town, turned into Broadway, swung the car into the curb. I got out and walked past a glittering window to a closed door. There was a little sign on the door: Closed on account of death. I rattled it, just the same.

A private dick, hired to guard the stuff in Barron's store, came and looked at me through the glass. He opened the door three inches.

"What do you want?" he said.

"I've got to see Mr. Morgan right away. It's important."

I flashed my badge at him. He unhooked the chain and let me in. He shut the door and locked it.

"Back in his private office."

I walked back. Morgan was sitting at his desk, resting his head on his hand. On the ash tray beside him smoke curled up from a cigar.

"Morgan," I said, "I'm arresting you for killing Sam Barron."

I guess he thought I was his guard. He jumped back, almost fell over his chair, terror and hate in his eyes.

"Y—you're crazy, man. Who are you?"

"Just a dick," I said. "See that box of cigars on your desk? You shouldn't smoke on a job like that, fella. Cigar ash and bits of tobacco are evidence. Stand up. I want to put the bracelets on you."

HE stared at me, his mouth twitching, his eyes out of focus. Suddenly he made a desperate lunge towards the drawer of his desk. I jumped and clipped him on the jaw, then turned in time to point my gun at the guard who had come running.

Morgan couldn't stand punishment. My punch hurt him and tears sprang into his eyes. He wilted, trembled and shook. The guard looked dumb, with his hands up. I put the cuffs on Morgan.

"Carry him out, fella," I said to the guard. "He's fainted on us."

"What are you going to do with him?" the guard asked.

"Give him to the cops for killing Barron."

I drove back to the hospital with Morgan beside me, all doubled up, pale, half-conscious and moaning. He revived some in the fresh air.

"Why'd you do it?" I said.

"He was cheating me, robbing me," he sobbed. "He was running a fence— and I was afraid the police— Oh, my God!"

He doubled up again, moaning.

I dragged him in and dropped him in front of Mike.

"Here's another guy that needs a doc," I said. "And he's the one you want for the Barron job."

"Morgan!" Mike said.

"That's his name," I a g r e e d. "Where's Marge?"

"She's in there with her brother," Dick said savagely. "The nurse let her in first. But I'm next and I'll make that rat cough up—"

Marge walked out, just then, dazed, with the nurse helping her. She saw me and her eyes seemed bigger than ever.

Her lips moved, but no words came out. After several trials, she said, "Stevie's dead! Stevie's dead!"

Dick, already heading for the door, began to cuss. I put my arm over the kid's shoulders and we sat down together. Dick came over and stood in front of us.

"Did he say where he put the stuff?" he yelled. "Don't try to hold out on me, sister, or—"

"Let the kid alone!" I snapped. "You start bothering her and I'll bust some knuckles right on your nose!"

"You're fired, Blake! I'll stand for just so much and—"

"Please, please!" Marge begged. "He told me. I'll tell you."

Dick made a grab for her arm.

"Don't say a word, Marge," I told her. "You can tell me—alone. But not this guy, not while he's acting so mean and ornery. Come on, kid. I'll take you home."

I helped her up and started for the door.

"You rat!" Dick said.

I paused at the door. "If you don't like the way I've handled this case, Mr. Hughes," I said, "I'll send my report to headquarters, to the big boss."

I had him stopped. He didn't have a word to say.

I took Marge home. I stayed with her until she fell asleep and then some more, because she was hanging on to my hand. If I could keep her hanging on to me, she wouldn't feel so lost and helpless, after the way Steve went out. I could—and did.

Morgan got life, Mona took a five-year jolt for another job they found out about, the chauffeur-dick got well, and Amy's trinkets were found just where Steve had told Marge—in the mattress in the room where Marge had found him.

That was that. Except that Dick Hughes got transferred and I got promoted. And Marge no longer dishes out hamburgers at the drive-in joint. No, she brings my steaks in on a big platter.

THE MAN IN AMBER GLASSES
By SAMUEL TAYLOR
Author of "Winterkill," etc.

The trouble wasn't that they were twins—it was Eddie being a rookie cop, and Tod being a killer!

Eddie tripped him, pulling at the hilt of the knife

IT rains in San Francisco like a bore talks — steadily, easily, without hurry—geared for the long pull; and oldtimers like Detective Captain John Malone swear the damp goes through rubber raincoats, through the skin and through the bones. The rain always put a cold finger on the sciatic nerve of Malone's right leg. This, and the appearance for the past week of hot money from the Ledbetter case, made his temper anything but long as he turned into a Howard street tavern and limped over to the gas circulator grill to warm his leg.

He was warming up, gently massaging his aching thigh when he began noticing the man with amber glasses at the bar. It was the amber glasses. They are worn for the sun, unless a man has very weak eyes—or unless for a disguise. The man was alone at the bar with a pink drink; probably a Singapore sling. The barkeep was reading a racing form spread on the cigar case near the window. It was mid afternoon, and dingy in the unlighted tavern. The man wore a tan trench coat with the collar high around his neck, a green hat, limp with wet, low over his forehead. Malone began hitching that way, out of the casual curiosity that had made him a good detective.

"Huh!" Malone snorted under his

breath, recognizing the man. It was young Tod Coates, promoted into plain clothes off a beat just last week. Tod Coates was supposed to be checking Third Street pawnshops right now, not lurking in taverns with a bum disguise and drinking Singapore slings.

"No, nothing for me." Malone waved back the barkeep.

"Okay, Captain. How's the lumbago?"

"Terrible, and it's sciatica." Malone put a hand on the shoulder of Coates' trench coat. "I'll have a little talk with you, boy."

The figure stiffened slightly under the hand, but the face kept straight ahead.

"About what?"

"You know what!"

Malone spoke tougher than he felt. Every young harness cop who goes up into the Detective Bureau gets the Sherlock Holmes complex for awhile—mastermind against crime, and all that. And Malone was a stickler for detail, cooperation, leg-work, routine. One straightening out was generally enough for a rookie detective.

"Okay," the young fellow said. He knocked Malone's hand away, jumped backwards, and shot with an automatic he had whipped from the pocket of his trench coat.

MALONE stumbled backwards and began going down, as much from surprise as from the force of the shot. The young fellow was running for the door. The barkeep stared stupidly, still leaning over the racing form on the cigar case.

"Hey!" The barkeep found voice when the man was almost to the door, then he flopped behind the counter as a bullet from the automatic shattered the glass bowl of a penny gum machine by his head.

The heavy roar of Malone's .38-Special revolver shook the glassware dis-play behind the counter, and the man in the trench coat went down, half out and half in the doorway. The automatic in his right hand hit the door glass and broke it, and sharp edges of the glass numbed his fingers so the weapon dropped onto the other side of the door.

Malone had gone to his knees. He used his right hand on the bar to get to his feet. His left arm was hanging loosely. He went over to the man in the trench coat.

"Just leave that gun be where it fell," he advised. He looked at the young fellow curiously. The amber glasses had fallen off, revealing weak pink-rimmed eyes, and on the man's left cheek was a birthmark the size of a half dollar. That wasn't young detective Tod Coates. Tod Coates didn't have that birthmark and he didn't have puffy pink-rimmed eyes. Unless Tod Coates was a crack hand at disguise. But this *couldn't* be Tod Coates; Tod Coates wouldn't have tried to shoot his way out.

"Okay, copper," the man grunted. "But how did you get wise?"

The barkeep's head showed above the cigar case. "I'll phone headquarters for you, Captain."

"No; get a taxi," Malone said. Searching the man, he had come upon a thick wallet, and he had a hunch.

At six twenty-five that afternoon, young Detective Tod Coates reported to Captain Malone's office. Malone had his left arm in a black sling. He squinted at Coates, extended a pair of amber glasses across the desk with his right hand. "Here, put these on." Then he kept squinting at Coates, and wagged his head wonderingly. "A twin brother," he muttered. "With a birthmark—"

"Yes, sir?"

"Sit down, Coates. Listen. A couple hours ago I nabbed a guy who served time in Sing Sing under the name of Eddie Jones. He's on parole from there now. He's new to this country. I'd never heard of him before I got the fingerprint report. He was toting a little over eight grand of the Ledbetter money."

"Well, that's fine, Captain!"

Malone grunted. "That's only half of it—a fifth of it. You know that every bill passed has been traced, and the gang hasn't spent much. If this Eddie Jones' cut was say ten grand, then there must be three or four others who got their slice."

Malone paused, made doodles on a scratch pad.

"Yes, sir."

Malone took a deep breath. "You know I'd give my right eye to bust this case and beat the G-Men to the punch. Cooperate, sure. But, still. . . . We've got this Eddie Jones guy under cover. He took a slug in the leg. He hasn't talked, and if I know anything about the type, he won't. We're working on him but I don't think it'll do any good. What I mean, he's smart. The smart ones can talk and not say anything. And he's tough. And—"

MALONE made more doodles. "Yes, sir," prompted Coates.

Malone sniffed blusteringly, glared at the young detective. "Look here, Coates, I'm not *asking* you to do this. You can make up your own mind. If you don't want to, okay. You know what sort of rats you'll be up against. You know the Ledbetter job. A week after they'd got the fifty grand, the rats drove by his house at night and tossed Ledbetter on the front lawn. What was left of him. They're that kind. You don't *have* to do it. It won't mean nothing to me—nothing against you—if you don't want to."

"Do what, Captain?"

"Let's go see this Eddie Jones, first.

I might be wrong."

Eddie Jones was on a bed in a hotel room. He had on his vest, shirt and tie, but no trousers. There were bandages on his right wrist and high on his left leg. He was lying there smoking a cigarette. Two detectives were in the room.

"Opened up?" Malone asked, coming in with Coates.

"Not yet," a detective said.

"Hello, Tod," the man on the bed said.

Tod Coates looked at the man for a matter of perhaps a minute. Malone and the two detectives were watching.

"Hello, Eddie," Tod Coates finally said. He grunted to Malone in explanation: "I knew him as a kid. We went to school together."

"Is that the way to treat a brother?" the man on the bed mocked.

"You're no brother of mine."

The man on the bed blew a puff of smoke. "Okay, Goodie Two Shoes. But I used to be."

Coates' lean face was a dull red color. There was fine sweat on the forehead. He turned to Malone, and said tightly: "I haven't seen this rat in over ten years. Not since we were kids."

"Goodie Two Shoes," jeered the man on the bed.

The two detectives were looking from one brother to the other. Malone's grizzled face showed nothing.

"That explains the resemblance, anyhow," the Captain grunted. "Come on, Coates."

Nothing was said until they were in the lobby. Coates felt the pressure of Malone's silence.

"We were twins," he explained. "There was always something wrong with Eddie. He was nervous. Bit his nails. Couldn't keep his hands off things. Late one night he came home and showed me a big roll of bills he'd got by slugging a drunk. I was going to make him take the money back, and he skipped out during the night. Took my clothes as well as his, and my savings bank. He was just a kid. The drunk died of brain concussion. I've never seen Eddie since."

"I never asked for that," Malone said. They went outside into the rain, Malone limping with his right leg. The neon lights were fuzzy in the wet.

"You never did say yes or no," Malone said.

Coates frowned. The shock of meeting Eddie had blown everything from his mind.

"About what?"

"The chances are this Eddie Jones is traveling with his pals. I've talked with the doctor, and he tells me it'll be simple to fake a birthmark and make the skin around your eyes puff out pink. You'd wear his amber glasses and his clothes, get a haircut like his. I've had a tailor clean his pants and fix the bullet holes. If you'd just wander around town like that, in the night spots, why, maybe— You know what getting this gang would mean to the Department— and to you. But I'm not *asking* you. You know what would happen if there was a hitch. And we couldn't give you a tail for protection. A tail might scare them off. If you want to say no—"

"I'll do it," Coates said.

"Well, maybe we'd better wait until we see if Eddie talks."

"I'll do it. I've got to do it. It'll sort of square up for him being my brother."

"You don't have to feel that way."

"Maybe not; but I do."

"Okay." Malone instantly was all business. "Now, look, Coates. All you do is try to find the hide-out. That's all. No Sherlock Holmes stuff. No brilliant gags. No gun battles. Or you'll end up in the bottom of the Bay with your feet in a tub of cement. If you can find the hide-out, that's enough. The Department will move in from there. You understand?"

"Yes, sir."

"Cooperation, Coates. Leave the brainwork to me."

WEARING Eddie's suit, tie, hat, shoes and trench coat, and a birthmark, Coates went around town. His eyes smarted, and it was a strain to see through the amber glasses. He dropped in at the Market street taverns, showed briefly at the Bal, the Redwood, Deauville, the Kit Kat, made a round of the big hotel cocktail rooms. It was near the closing hour, and he was in a dive south of Market when a man came alongside him at the bar.

"What's the matter, Squint?"

"Matter with what?"

"You know that deal's on. Why didn't you show up at Lou's?"

Coates didn't say anything.

"Ross sent me out looking. You run into anything wrong?"

"No."

"Well, come on."

"As soon as I've finished this sling."

"You've had too many slings. I've tailed you in four joints as it is."

Coates was glad no shadow had been put on him. He went with the man out to a tan car. The man was short and slim, with a hatchet face. He had a little daub of black moustache under a sharp nose. He drove a circuitous route, watching in the rear view mirror for possible pursuit. The rain rattled against the sloping windshield and the wiper scraped with a dry scratching sound.

The man said, "It's lucky about this deal. That Ledbetter dough is still plenty hot. Me, personal, I've been plenty nervous since we had to dip into it."

"Ye-ah," said Coates.

"Dodge only offers twenty per cent cash," the man said. "But Ross figures we can jack him up twenty-five. That'll be okay with me. I'll turn over my cut of the hot stuff for twenty-five per cent safe dough any time."

"Sure."

The man drove zig-zag for awhile longer, then cut through the city towards North Beach.

"What's the matter with you, Squint?"

Coates gripped the automatic in the pocket of the trench coat.

"What do you mean, what's the matter with me?"

"You're quiet. That ain't like you."

"I'm thinking."

"Ye-ah, it's enough to make a man think. I ain't felt so good myself since we had to dip into the hot stuff. It's a good thing Ross is swinging this deal with Dodge to get rid of it."

And lucky Malone bumped into Eddie when he did, Coates thought. If the gang had got rid of the hot money the trail would have ended.

"Here we are." The hatchet-faced man swung the car into the basement garage of an apartment house built into the steep slope of Telegraph hill. They took an elevator, and the thin-faced man gave four spaced raps on a door at the end of a corridor. The number on the door was 401. A blonde girl opened the door.

"I found him, Lou."

The girl said, "It's about time. Ross is getting nervous."

There were three men around a table in the room. They had coats off and shirt cuffs turned back. Coates didn't know any of them. They were playing cards. The tallest of the three laid down his hand and said, "What the hell's the matter with you, Squint?"

"Nothing's the matter with me."

"Dodge won't hold the deal open forever. And I got a hunch we'd better fly. You didn't pass no more of that hot stuff when you was out, did you?"

"No."

THERE were four bottles on the table. The tall man poured himself two fingers of rye into a tumbler and threw it off.

The blonde girl said, "Ross, go easy on that stuff."

"You shut up." The tall man wiped his mouth with his sleeve. He was well built, with sleek brown hair and regular features. A handsome man. Maybe a bit too good looking.

He said, "Okay, then let's have the dough, all of you, and I'll take it to Dodge." And to Coates: "I upped him to twenty-five percent while you was gone."

The other three men tossed wallets on the table. Ross checked the contents of each. It made a thick sheaf.

Ross looked up at Coates. "Well, Squint?"

"I don't know about this deal with Dodge," Coates sparred. He had hold of the automatic in the pocket of his trench coat. One thing of Eddie's he wasn't carrying—the eight thousand of hot money. Neither he nor Malone had seen a possible use for that. Coates gripped the automatic, and wondered what chance he'd have trying to face down the four men with it. The hatchet-faced man was behind him, and the girl was over by the door. He didn't like the idea of showing a gun in this company. These men faced death on apprehension; they'd show fight to resist capture. And Coates remembered Malone's admonition — don't try to be smart, don't try any tricks. Just find the hide-out and notify the department.

All eyes were on him. Ross came up from his chair. He was half a head taller than Coates. He said, "What's the matter with you, sourpuss?"

"Let him talk, Ross," the hatchet-faced man suggested. "What's your gripe, Squint?"

"How do we know this deal is okay?" Coates sparred.

The thin-faced man groaned. "Always suspicious!"

"A hell of a time to be pulling that!" Ross snarled. "How do you know you're alive? Dodge is all right, or else nobody is."

"Sure; but why should he want to buy hot money? What'll he do with it?" Coates objected. "And remember there's a reward on us, if somebody wanted it."

"Dodge is okay, you poor sap," Ross said acidly. "If he buys the hot stuff, what the hell do we care what he does with it? He can hold it a few years, maybe. Or he can run it out through his bookie joints. You can't trace that kind of dough."

Coates knew who Dodge was, now. Dodge ran a cigar store on Eddy street, openly. He was suspected of running some other things. If he could get this gang, and in addition catch Dodge in the act of buying hot money— But one thing at a time. And what was facing him now was his lack of Eddie's cut of the money. Ross was suspicious.

"Well, Squint?" Ross asked.

Coates took one of the four bottles, poured himself a drink and threw it off. He needed it.

"What's the matter with you, Squint?" one of the men asked. "At noon you was all for this deal, and now—"

"Shut up," Ross growled at the man. And then, suddenly switching to a friendliness that maybe was a shade too sweet: "Sure, Squint. Have it your own way. If you don't want to go in on the deal, why, you don't have to."

"I don't get it," objected the little hatchet-faced man. "If one of us is still passing the hot stuff, and he's traveling with the others—"

"Shut up, Peanut," Ross advised. "If I say it's okay, then it's okay. Or would you want to make something out of it?"

"I just had a idea," the thin-faced man mumbled.

COATES was getting an idea. He shrugged. "Okay, count me in. Peanut is right. We all ought to go in on the deal, for self-protection. But I'll have to go get my dough."

"Got to get it?" Peanut piped. "Say, what—?"

"Where is it, Squint?" Ross asked. Ross' voice was soft, almost gentle.

"I thought a dick was tailing me, so I bought a thirty-nine cent zipper bag in a drug store and checked it at a night club."

"Eight grand in a zipper bag?" one of the men gasped. "You got plenty of faith in check girls!"

"What else could I do?" Coates asked. "I thought a dick was tailing me."

"Why, sure, Squint," Ross said genially. "What else could you do if you thought a dick was on your tail? I'll go with you, Squint, and we'll pick it up on our way to see Dodge."

Coates didn't like the pseudo-friendliness of Ross' manner. But if he got Ross outside—

"Get my hat and coat, Squint, and we'll go," Ross said.

There were four doors in the room. Coates knew one led to the hallway. Ross' coat and hat would be in one of the rooms leading from the other three doors. Coates could feel something behind Ross' friendly manner. Suspicion. Maybe some little item of the impersonation— Coates knew Ross was leader of the gang. He didn't dare refuse to get the hat and coat. Three doors.

Coates took another slug of Scotch, neat, to stall for time while he tried to be casual about examining the three doors. The liquor burned a warm path down his gullet. The one door had a glass plate instead of a knob. That obviously was a swinging door leading to the kitchen. Of the two doors to the north, one was six inches shorter and a bit narrower than the other. The bigger door would lead to a bedroom. The smaller to a closet—or a bathroom. But the bathroom generally lead off from the bedroom. Coates went to the smaller door.

It was a closet.

Wraps were inside, on hangers hanging from a rod. Three hats were on a shelf above the rod. Ross had crossed to the closet behind him. There was a printed paper in a frame under glass screwed to the inside of the closet door. It said, "Sutter Apartments, Rules and Regulations." Each rule and regulation was numbered. There were ten of them. Ross was the tallest man of the gang. Coates took the longest coat from the hanger.

"Here you go, Ross."

"Thanks, Squint."

The coat was blue gabardine. Of the three hats on the shelf, one was brown, one gray, and one blue. Coates reached for the blue hat.

A million stars exploded in his head.

He regained consciousness on a lounge. The lounge had red leather upholstery and arms of nickeled pipe. The four men and the girl were looking at him. The left side of his face was cool. Ross had a bit of cotton in one hand and a bottle of rubbing alcohol in the other. Ross evidently had worked on the fake birthmark. Coates knew the game was up.

"Where's Squint?" Ross asked.

Coates tried a forlorn bluff. "You trying to get my cut? Is that it?"

Ross hit him in the face. "None of that. Where's Squint?"

"I'm Squint. I'm Eddie. What the hell?"

Ross hit him again. "No go, Ringer. I spotted something funny about you when you came in. Didn't know what. One thing, you was awful quiet, for Squint. And then you took a drink of Scotch, and Squint hates Scotch. You poured with your right hand instead of your left. And then I noticed your hand. Squint keeps his nails chewed halfway down to the moons. Little things, Ringer."

COATES felt like a fool. Malone might have overlooked the small detail; but Coates had known that Eddie chewed his nails as a boy, and that's a habit that is hard to break.

The men held a council at the far end of the room. Ross crossed to the lounge, pulled Coates up, took him to the table and shoved him in a chair. The girl brought paper and a pencil.

"You're a copper," Ross said. "The cops have got Squint. You're going to write a note to get Squint loose. Who would you write it to?"

Coates was having a very small idea. "Detective Captain Malone," he said. "Malone is keeping Squint under cover."

"Write this and nothing else: 'Dear Malone, They have got me and they'll kill me inside an hour unless you let Eddie Jones loose. And give Eddie his money.' . . . Okay; now sign it."

Coates signed it, "Tod Rettus," and prayed silently.

"He might try to pull a gag," Peanut said.

Ross studied the note. He gave it to Peanut. Peanut handed it to another man. They all examined it. Coates was afraid to breathe. He took another slug of Scotch.

"Peanut, go out away from here and give somebody five bucks to deliver this to Captain Malone," Ross directed, putting the note in an envelope. "Don't let the guy get a good look at you."

"Maybe Eddie will be tailed," Peanut objected.

"Not Squint. Squint knows how."

Peanut went out.

One of the men drew an automatic.

"Put that away," Ross said.

"We ain't going to let this guy go now he knows us?"

"We won't let him go; but we've got to use him to get Squint. Maybe this won't work, and we'll have to try something else. We got to get Squint sprung. They'll work on him. We got to spring him before he sings."

Ross tied Coates. Lashed ankles, and tied arms across the chest with a hitch on the wrists and the knot in the middle of the back. He slugged Coates in the face, carried him into the bedroom and threw him on the bed. One of the men stayed in the bedroom with him. This man was of stubby build, with protruding ears. There was a steel-sash casement window by the bed. A roof evidently was near the window, for there came the soft rattle of falling rain. Coates lay there on the bed and let his mind run in a circle.

The captives hadn't caught onto the trick in the note. Maybe Malone wouldn't. Of course Malone had the advantage of knowing the detective's name. Maybe Malone would let Eddie loose and maybe he wouldn't. Maybe—

"Just lay still, copper," the stubby man advised.

Coates quit trying to reach the knot in the center of his back. The rain kept rattling softly outside the window on the invisible roof. The stubby man would look at his wrist watch every little while, drum his fingers on his knee. When he had looked at his watch a couple of dozen times he got out a cigarette and lighted it.

"I'm cutting down to one every half hour," he said. "I'm trying to quit."

"A man likes to break a bad habit."

"Yes, I—say, are you trying to kid me, copper?"

The stubby man finished his cigarette then began looking at his watch, drumming his fingers on a knee. Finally he lighted another cigarette.

Four measured knocks came faintly.

"There's Squint." The stubby man went out the door, leaving it open. "Hello, Squint! How's your fingernails?"

COATES began worming across the bed towards the window.

"Let me at that guy," growled Eddie's voice.

"He can wait a couple minutes," Ross' voice said. "Nobody tailed you, Squint?"

"No; I know my stuff. I come here in three taxis and passed through a theater and a couple of alleys meanwhile. My leg's giving me hell. So Goodie Two Shoes tried to ring in for me, huh? Let me at that guy!"

"He can wait awhile, Squint. How about the dough?"

"They give it to me. We'll gossip later."

"Wait a minute, Squint. Listen, did you sing?"

"What the hell do you think I am? Did I sing!"

In the bedroom, Coates had reached the window.

"You didn't sing at all?" persisted Ross' voice.

"Say, listen—now, wait a minute, Ross."

Coates could see nothing but blackness out the wet window. His back was to the steel casement, his fingertips just touching the handle of the latch. His weight against the window held the latch fast, and if he eased the weight he couldn't reach the latch handle. He could hear the rain on the roof outside. Was it close to the window or a story down? Would there be an alley between the buildings? This was the fourth floor. . . . Coates figured he'd have to take a chance. Malone evidently hadn't read the note right, or he would be here before now.

Through the open door there came the sudden sound of scuffle, a strangled scream. Then silence, and a voice breaking through hollowly.

"Why'd you do that for, Ross?"

"The coppers know he was in the Ledbetter job, you fool. We can't let him tag with us after he's known."

"Then why'd you spring him?"

"To make sure he wouldn't sing. And to get his cut."

"Well, I guess that's right, Ross."

Eddie staggered into view in the doorway. The handle of a knife was sticking from his side. He leaned against the door jamb, breathing heavily. His amber glasses were directed at Coates, who was fighting to get the casement catch loose against the pressure of his body.

Ross appeared, yelled, ran through the doorway reaching for his gun. Eddie tripped him, fell heavily on him, pulling at the hilt of the knife.

"Hurry, Tod. Hurry," Eddie gasped.

The catch moved and Coates fell backwards into the blackness. Then something caught his heels and the back of his head swung down and around and hit the stucco wall with all the noise of an avalanche. The cuff of his trousers or the cords at his ankles had caught something, probably that infernal catch. The blow had stunned him. He was helpless. Then somebody was dragging him back up by the legs and he was doing his best to kick loose.

"Keep still, you fool!" roared the voice of Detective Captain Malone.

"D'you want to fall four floors down to that alley?"

THERE was one more bit of business that night—the trapping of Dodge. Dodge was caught in the act of receiving the Ledbetter money from the man he thought was Eddie Jones.

"Say, there was a night's work!" Captain Malone said to Coates when they were riding back in a police car. "Coates, you're all right! That note, it was clever!"

"I still don't get it," a detective said.

"He signed it 'Tod Rettus.' I knew it was from him by the 'Tod,' and because nobody else knew about Eddie Jones. And I knew it was the Sutter apartments by the 'Rettus.' I had a guy on each floor and when the guy on the fourth floor saw Eddie go in number 401 he signaled to us across the street and we come up."

"I get it. Rettus; Sutter," the detective admitted. "But how did you know it wasn't Sutter *street?*"

"Hell! A bright lad like Tod Coates, if it had been a place on Sutter *street,* why, he'd of found some way to give the address! . . . You're all right, Tod. You'll get something out of this, and that's a promise. You're the kind of a man I like. Initiative! Courage! Brains! I like to see a man who can think and act for himself!"

Ordinarily, such a statement from Malone would have startled Tod Coates, but he wasn't listening. He was thinking of Eddie. Eddie tripping Ross. Eddie saying, "Hurry, Tod. Hurry." He had never felt good about Eddie, but now he felt some better.

MY FATHER—MURDERER

By RUSSELL GRAY

Author of "Daughters of Lusting Torment," etc.

She fought like a wildcat

It was Detective-Sergeant Allen Fisk's job to bring in that murderer—even though the fiend be his own father!

THE theatres were disgorging their audiences when Detective-Sergeant Allen Fisk made his way with easy strides through Forty-Fourth Street to the little hotel on Eighth Avenue where he lived. He was passing the last theatre on the block when a shrill voice exclaimed almost in his ear: "Oh, daddy, buy me one of those."

Instinctively he turned his head and found himself looking at a cute little brunette with a sable wrap over her brief evening gown. She had stopped with one tiny foot on the running-board of a taxi and her black eyes danced merrily as they looked up at Fisk. A man held one of her elbows.

Fisk said to the man: "Hello, Dad."

The brunette started to giggle. She thought it was a snappy retort. Then abruptly she was silent and looked from her escort to Fisk and a frown creased her ivory smooth forehead.

The two men looked very much alike —the same tall, lean figures, the same blunt features and unflinching gray eyes. Except that her escort was considerably older and softer. Dissipation and easy living had raised puffy balls under his eyes and his skin was tinged with yellow.

The older man held out a hand. "Well, Son, I haven't seen you for some time."

"No," the detective said. He looked down again at the brunette, but he didn't smile. "It seems we don't move in the same social set."

The older man laughed. "My son doesn't approve of me," he explained to the girl. "He's a cop and thinks his old man is a reprobate. And wipe that worshipful look off your face, sweetheart, because he's a very moral and clean-living young man."

THE girl formed an O with her lips and kept her eyes fixed on Allen Fisk. A female voice from inside the taxi called out impatiently: "For crying out loud, Wilber, step on it!"

A man's head poked through the open door of the taxi. The face was handsome save for a feeble chin which undermined the other features. In the shadows within the cab Allen Fisk made out a girl with blonde curls leaning forward in the seat in order to get a look at him.

"Well, if it isn't the Boy Scout son!" the man in the taxi sneered.

Allen Fisk knew him. It was his job to know men like Gordon Swenson who owned pieces of some of the hottest spots in New York.

The brunette at last found her voice. "You've been holding out on us, Wilber, darling. You never told us you had a handsome son. Let's take him along."

"Sure," Wilber Fisk agreed heartily. "How about it, Allen? Join us in a party."

The brunette tucked a hand intimately through Allen Fisk's arm. "I'm going to like you."

The detective gently disengaged her hand from his arm. He said: "I go in for slumming only in the line of duty." Then he said to his father: "How about coming with me, Dad? We haven't had an evening together in months."

Wilber Fisk grinned. "Still trying to reform your old man, eh?"

"Why waste time on the Boy Scout?" Gordon Swenson snapped from the taxi.

Behind them other cabs were impatiently blowing their horns. A patrolman came up. "Hey, you, get going." Then he saw Allen Fisk and his scowl faded. "Oh, it's you, Sergeant. Anything up?"

"I was talking to my father," Allen Fisk said in a dull voice. "Sorry."

Wilber Fisk shook his son's hand and got into the cab after the brunette. As the cab pulled out, Allen Frisk could see the brunette seated on his father's lap. She was waving at him through the back window.

"Not bad for a buck his age," the patrolman commented pleasantly. He was grinning broadly.

Allen Fisk said nothing. He spun on his heels and continued to his hotel.

For some time he lay wide awake in bed. He thought of his mother and father as they had been until five years ago—a loving, faithful, understanding couple aging gracefully. His mother had believed that the world revolved about her husband and his father hadn't had eyes for any other woman in the world.

Then she had died, and for three years Wilber Fisk hadn't much cared whether he stayed on earth or not. Two years ago he sold his small manufacturing concern and announced his retirement. He had money, not much, but enough to spend his remaining years playing around. Only he did the wrong kind of playing. It was as if he were now trying to sow the wild oats his faithfulness to his wife had prevented him from sowing in the past.

Allen Fisk couldn't find it in his heart to condemn his father altogether. The tragedy of his wife's death and the terrible loneliness which followed had undermined him. He thought he was getting fun out of life. Well, maybe. It wasn't the fun his father might be having that Allen Fisk disapproved of. It was the fact that his father was making himself ridiculous; was being played for a sucker, a sugar-daddy.

He needs a good spanking, Allen Fisk thought; and smiled wearily and fell asleep.

THE jangling of the telephone woke him abruptly. He reached for the phone without moving more than his arm.

"Allen?" an anxious voice said.

"Yeah." Then Allen Fisk sat up a couple of inches. "Oh, hello, Dad. Your voice sounds so strange I didn't recognize it."

"Listen, Son — I just killed a woman."

For a second there was no sound on either end of the line. When Allen Fisk at last spoke there was a catch in his voice.

"This is no time for a joke, Dad."

"I wish to heaven it were a joke. But she's dead, I tell you, and I killed her. God knows I didn't mean to. She had that gun and I tried to take it away from her and there was a shot. What'll I do now, Son? The cops'll be after me any minute."

Allen Fisk said quietly: "Start from the beginning, Dad."

"All right. After we left you we went up to Swenson's apartment. Had drinks and all the rest—you know. Then after a while Swenson and Emily disappeared into another room—I think

it was the library—and then—"

"Which one's Emily—the brunette?"

"No, the blonde. Emily Martin. I was on the couch with the other one— Hazel Griffin. She was acting strangely; kept looking at the library door. Suddenly she jumped up and ran to a desk and pulled out a gun and made for the door. I knew then that she'd gone mad with jealousy of Swenson—I thought she'd cared a little for me. Damn her, after all I gave her I imagined—"

"Never mind that," Allen Fisk said. "You should have known bettter. What happened then?"

"I knew she was going to kill Emily or Swenson or both, so I threw myself at her and tried to take the gun away from her. She fought like a wild cat. And then—then the gun went off. Hazel went down without a sound. What happened after that I'm not sure. Swenson and Emily came in and I was standing there with the gun in my hand staring down at the blood on her forehead. Those two just looked at me with horror and said nothing. I knew they'd call the police. I became panic-stricken. I dropped the gun and made for the door. I didn't even wait for the elevator but ran down the stairs. And that's—that's all."

Sweat plastered Allen Fisk's pajamas to his body. He asked: "How long ago did that happen?"

"About an hour, I think. But I've lost all sense of time. I roamed the streets, not knowing what to do. I thought of coming to you—but you're a cop, Son."

"Yes," Allen Fisk said. There was a tight knot in the pit of his stomach. "Yes, I'm a cop."

What was he first, he thought, a cop or the son of his father? If his father had come up here, would he have turned him in?

He asked: "Where are you now, Dad?"

A bitter chuckle came over the wire. "Still the cop, eh? Well, I'm in a booth and it's a dial phone. I'm leaving, son. Chances are we'll never again see each other. That's why I phoned you. I'm saying good-bye."

"Dad, maybe we can work this out. There's no case against you. You tried to get the gun away from her."

AGAIN that bitter chuckle came over the wire. "It's no good, Son. I can see the D. A.'s case now. The girl was going to throw me over. I hadn't any money left. You see, she'd taken me to the cleaners. I'd told that to Hazel Griffin the day before and she must have told Emily Martin and Swenson. That was to be our last party. Don't you see the set-up? They'll say I killed her because she'd milked me and then was going to throw me over."

"Yes," Allen Fisk said dully.

"But I didn't kill her intentionally. That's another reason I phoned. I didn't want you to go through life thinking you are the son of a murderer. You believe me, don't you, Son?"

"Yes, Dad."

"Don't think too harshly of me. I know you're thinking I brought it on myself. I've a couple of thousand left —enough to get away on. . . . Well, good-bye."

"Dad!"

There was a click and the line was dead.

Allen Fisk cradled the phone with unsteady hands. Stripping off his pajamas he wiped his sweat-covered body with a towel, then dressed.

As he opened the door, DeLany, a first-grade detective in his own squad, was coming up the hall.

DeLany said: "Hello, Sergeant. May I come in?"

Allen Fisk let DeLany enter the two-room hotel apartment first, then followed. DeLany's eyes moved about the room. He strolled into the bathroom, then into the bedroom. Fisk did not follow. He heard his closet door open and shut.

When DeLany returned to the living room, Fisk asked: "Are you on duty?"

DeLany nodded. "Can you tell me the last time you saw your father?"

"What's up?"

"Sorry, Sergeant, but I'm supposed to be asking the questions."

Fisk said: "I saw him at about eleven-thirty this evening. He was coming out of the 'Make Mine Baloney' revue and he was with Gordon Swenson and a couple of girls. They were going up to Swenson's apartment."

"And you haven't seen or heard from him since?"

Fisk picked a pack of cigarettes off a table and offered one to DeLany and took one for himself. When the cigarettes were lit he said:

"My father phoned me about fifteen minutes ago. I don't know where from. I was on the way to Swenson's apartment when you met me."

He was too good a detective not to know that it was dangerous to lie about facts which could be verified. Perhaps the switchboard operator in the hotel had listened in to the conversation. And he couldn't give his father's version of what had happened without telling that he had spoken to him.

DeLany regarded the tip of his cigarette. "Where is he now?"

"I told you I don't know."

DeLany kept looking at his cigarette. Fisk asked: "Who's on the case?"

"Captain Rasmussen himself."

"And he thinks that I might be hiding my father out?"

"Well—" DeLany said.

Allen Fisk started for the door. "Let's go to Swenson's," he said.

GORDON SWENSON lived in a swanky apartment house on Madison Avenue. Fisk stopped in the living room doorway and looked at the pathetic little body on the floor. The rouge on her face stood out in ghastly contrast to her chalk-white skin. She was quite young; Fisk hadn't realized how young she really was when he had seen her earlier that evening. Not more than twenty—and his father was nearly three times that age!

Captain Rasmussen, tall and lean and gray-haired, was talking to Dr. Hall, the chubby, bald Medical Examiner. Rasmussen's head bobbed up and down toward Fisk, his expression serious, grim. He beckoned to DeLany and the two went to the other end of the room where they stood talking for a couple of minutes in undertones.

Then the captain came over to Fisk. "Sorry about this business, Sergeant. This is murder, you know, and your job is to catch murderers."

"I don't know where my father is," Fisk said. "DeLany told you I didn't."

"That's what *you* told him."

Allen Fisk met the captain's eyes squarely. "That's the God's honest truth. My father phoned me so that I would know what really happened. He didn't tell me from where. You see"— his tone became tinged with bitterness —"he didn't trust me either."

"Did he tell you he was hiding out? Did he tell you where?"

Fisk said: "No."

He could see disbelief in Rasmussen's probing eyes. The captain turned to DeLany. "Find out where Wilber Fisk banked his money. This girl cleaned him out, but maybe he has some left. He'll try to withdraw it tomorrow to make a getaway."

DeLany said: "Yes, sir," and left.

Fisk knew how Rasmussens' mind worked. Rasmussen figured that he, Allen Fisk, would try to get in touch with his father to warn him not to go near a bank. Detectives would be constantly

on his tail; his hotel wire would be tapped.

Rasmussen said grimly: "He hasn't got a chance of getting away. He's got a tuxedo on; ran out without a hat or coat. We know he didn't go to his own apartment. His outfit will make him conspicuous. He'll try to buy a suit or maybe swap the tuxedo for different clothes. We have that angle covered too."

"I tried to talk him into coming in," Allen Fisk said. "Because you can't pin a charge on him. The girl, Hazel Griffin, snatched the gun out of that desk drawer and was making for the library where Swenson and Emily Martin were. It seems she was only playing my father for a sucker and was jealous of the Martin girl. My father tried to take the gun away from her and in the struggle it accidently went off."

"Is that your father's story?"

"It's the truth," Allen Fisk said. "Then he became panic-stricken and ran out. You'll find the girl's prints on the gun."

CAPTAIN RASMUSSEN smiled mirthlessly. "There are no prints on the gun. Your father wiped them off."

Fisk's eyes went wide. "He was scared," he faltered. "Desperate. He didn't know what he was doing."

"Didn't he?" Rasmussen said. "He knew enough to fire a second shot into the girl when she was on the ground and then wipe the gun."

"A second shot?" Fisk said. His legs felt like rubber. "There couldn't have been."

Rasmussen turned to Dr. Hall. "Tell him what you just told me."

The M.E. expelled a cloud of cigaret smoke. He said: "The girl was shot twice. The first bullet grazed her forehead and buried itself in that wall. It knocked her unconscious. Then when she lay on the floor a second bullet was sent into her heart. The gun was fired from about six inches away directly above her."

Allen Fisk felt numb all over. He stared stupidly at Rasmussen, then at Dr. Hall.

"And both shots were heard by Swenson and Emily Martin who were in the other room," Rasmussen told him. "When they came in here they saw your father wiping the gun with a handkerchief and staring down at her and muttering: 'Damn you, you had it coming to you!' Then when he saw the two he dropped the gun and ran."

Allen Fisk muttered: "No, there's something wrong. Dad wouldn't have lied to me. And he couldn't commit deliberate murder if his life depended on it."

"He had plenty of motive," Rasmussen pointed out. "The girl had bled him white and was going to throw him over. This was their last date together. Swenson says your father was almost crazy at the thought of losing her. He pleaded with her and at one time he started blubbering like a baby. You're in homicide, Sergeant, and I don't have to tell you that given enough provocation and opportunity there's not a person who couldn't murder. I know it's a blow to you, but"—he shrugged—"you might as well face it."

Face the fact that his father had murdered a defenseless girl in cold blood! Fisk's eyes, which could be grim and utterly merciless when facing a brutal killer, now looked something like those of a scared rabbit.

Captain Rasmussen went to a window and stood looking out. Dr. Hall silently left the room. They're feeling sorry for me, Allen Fisk thought numbly. Sorry for the son whose father is a murderer.

As in a dream he moved out of the apartment. Reporters were milling in the hall, crowding about Gordon Swenson and Emily Martin.

The blonde was holding a lace handkerchief to her eyes while flashlight bulbs flared. She was gasping: "It was a brutal murder by a jealous old man who wanted Hazel to throw herself away on him. When she refused, he shot her. Poor Hazel! She was the best friend any girl ever had."

Allen Fisk had glimpsed her only once before in the dim light of the taxi. Now he saw that she was a hard, overpainted blonde long past her prime.

"I hope they catch him at once and give him the chair," she said to the reporters. "Maybe I am vindictive, but it will be a lesson to those rich old lechers who think—"

"Shut up!"

THE words exploded from Allen Fisk's throat involuntarily. He went toward the girl with clenched fists. Reporters made a path for him. The girl cast a scared glance at him and clutched at Swenson.

"What you're saying about my father is a lie and you know it," Allen Fisk said. "You and that other girl and all the rest like you—you drain men not only of their money but of their souls. You—!"

He started to lift one hand. The girl screamed and Swenson, white-faced, moved to step between her and Fisk. A hand fell on Fisk's shoulder and a detective named Williams whispered in his ear: "Easy, Sergeant. Take it easy."

Fisk's upraised hand fell weakly to his side. He was making a fool of himself. About him the reporters and photographers were going crazy with excitement. This would be in all the morning papers; there would be photos of him about to strike the girl.

Allen Fisk wheeled and made for the stairs. Reporters tried to stop him;

they hurled questions at him, clamored for a statement. Without a word he brushed through them. His face was a mask on which lines of mental anguish were etched.

By the time he reached the street, he had shaken off the last of the reporters. He started to walk. He didn't know where he was going. He didn't care. Somewhere in the city his father was hiding. Penniless, without the craftiness of the hardened criminal, he hadn't a chance. There would be a sensational trial and finally that moment when Wilber Fisk was strapped into the electric chair.

There was no hope that it would turn out any other way. This was deliberate, cold blooded—

Allen Fisk stopped abruptly. His heart started racing. He lit a cigaret in order to steady his nerves. A haze lifted from his mind, and only keen perception remained.

Then he was moving again, rapidly. Once again he was the professional hunter of murderers.

It was several minutes past four o'clock when Allen Fisk strode into a bar-and-grill on Seventh Avenue. He swept the bar with his eyes, then went up to a short fat man who was hunched over the bar fingering a highball and reading a morning paper. Fisk looked over his shoulder. The story of Hazel Griffin's murder was headlined. There were photos of Hazel Griffin and of Gordon Swenson and a big one of Wilber Fisk. A sub-headline said: SUSPECT IS FATHER OF N. Y. DETECTIVE. Allen Fisk felt a lump in his throat.

He tapped the fat man who looked up lazily. Then the fat man jumped off the seat.

"I've just been reading about your old man, Sergeant. I'm sorry as hell."

There were only three or four people at the bar, but they all turned to look at him. Fisk said: "Let's sit at a table."

The fat man picked up his drink and paper and waddled to a corner table. Fisk took the paper from him and read about the murder. The edition had gone to press too soon after the murder to contain any information. There were, however, the addresses of the principal people involved. Fisk jotted them down. The fat man kept eyeing him curiously.

FINALLY Allen Fisk said: "Waldo, you're a no good booze hound who lives on his mother and has never done an honest day's work. But you know everything there is to know about Broadway. Who and what is Emily Martin?"

"One of the girls. Musical shows in her youth. She's through now; getting old. Hasn't worked in a couple of years. Feeds on men."

"Principally G o r d o n Swenson?" Fisk asked.

Waldo nodded. "She'd like to make a permanent thing of it. Only there's too much youth available for Swenson to agree with her."

"And what about Hazel Griffins?"

"She worked in a couple of night club choruses. Young and good to look at. Came from the sticks less than two years ago. But she knew how to separate a Wall Streeter from his bankroll better than—" Waldo stopped. "I'm sorry I said that, Sergeant. I wasn't thinking. I guess your old man was all right, only a little naive."

"Yes," Allen Fisk said. "How did Hazel feel about Swenson?"

Waldo spread his fingers on the table. "I don't know everything. I've seen them around together, but one sees Swenson around with a lot of young stuff."

"But mostly with Emily Martin?"

"That's right."

The detective stood up. "Thanks, Waldo," he said.

He got into a taxi in front of the place and gave the driver one of the addresses he had copied out of the newspaper. Through the back window he could see that he was being followed by another cab. He shrugged. That must be the man Captain Rasmussen had put on his tail.

His taxi stopped in front of an apartment house on West End Avenue. The other cab stopped down the block. Fisk paid the bill and stepped into the doorway of the apartment. Then he stepped out again and saw a man emerge from the second taxi. It looked like Williams. Fisk smiled and went to the elevator.

His heart was beating like a trip-hammer when he pressed the button of a fifth floor apartment. Here's your chance, Dad, he breathed. Your last chance.

A woman's voice called: "Who's there?"

"The police."

The voice took on a frightened tinge. "What do you want? I told you everything I know."

"Sure. But there are a couple of questions more. It'll take only a minute."

He heard a lock turn. The door opened a couple of inches. Then there was a little screech and the door started to close. He put his shoulder against the door and it flew open.

Emily Martin retreated before him, crying, "Get out of here! Don't you dare touch me!"

Fisk didn't move toward her. He said gravely: "I came to apologize, Miss Martin. I lost my head in the hall. You see, at that time I wasn't sure that my father was the murderer."

He stood in the door of the living room. As he talked his eyes flicked about. No sign of Gordon Swenson.

Had he left immediately after he had taken her home?

Emily Martin looked puzzled. "Sure your father killed her. Maybe I shouldn't have spoken the way I did, but Emily was my best friend."

FISK nodded stupidly. "I can't understand how Dad could have done it. But now since his suicide and the note . . ."

"Suicide?" the woman said, her watery blue eyes fixed on his face.

"He killed himself," Fisk choked out. "We got the word at headquarters a few minutes ago. He left a note behind confessing that he had shot Hazel Griffin." He sighed. "I guess that was the best way out for him."

The woman expelled her breath. Was it a sigh of relief? Was that a flicker of a smile he saw on her lips?

Fisk said: "In the note he told how it was just the way you and Swenson said it happened. He shot her once in the temple. Then when he saw that she wasn't quite dead, he leaned over and put a slug in her heart. Then he carefully wiped the prints off the gun and fled. He told it just like that in his suicide note."

The woman's mouth half opened and stayed like that. Bewilderment leaped into her eyes, then fear.

"Say!" she b l u r t e d. Then she checked herself. She turned her back to him and went to a table for a cigaret. Fisk stood looking at her back, at the way her shoulders slumped suddenly, at the way her hand shook as she applied the match to the cigaret.

Then he laughed aloud. He felt suddenly fine.

The woman whirled. Her face was ugly with fear.

"Damn you!" she said. "Get out of here!"

Still laughing, he strode over to her and grasped her hand roughly.

"I knew it would work. You're jittery as hell. Too much liquor, too fast a life—your nerves are shot. You can't keep it in you. And now you've confessed."

"It's a lie!" she cried. "I never said I killed Hazel. You're trying to frame me."

"Either you or Swenson killed her," Fisk said. "If it was Swenson, you're an accessory after the fact, which rates a twenty year term in this state. You can save yourself by talking."

A red tongue flicked over her lips. She gulped. She started to open her mouth.

"I wouldn't if I were you, Emily," a voice said softly behind Allen Fisk. "Although I don't see that it really matters."

Fisk whirled, his hand jerking up to his shoulder. Gordon Swenson stood in the bedroom doorway, a blue automatic pointed coolly at Fisk's heart. Fisk dropped his hand, cursing himself. He should have taken the trouble to look into the bedroom.

"It's dangerous pointing guns at detectives," he said drily.

A cocky smile spread over Swenson's handsome features. "Not this detective. Plenty of witnesses heard you threaten Emily Martin. When you were stopped from striking her, you rushed out into the street like a wild man. After roaming around you came up to her apartment to beat her up because of what she had said about your old man. I happened to be here. We struggled and you were, unfortunately"—his voice dropped—"shot."

The woman backed slowly away from Fisk. "Gordon, you're not going to—"

"I don't know how much you know, Fisk," Swensen said. "It can't be more than a hunch; I'm sure you have no evidence. But you have enough influence to get Emily down to your damned torture chambers and sweat the truth out of her. You're right, she'll break, and I'm not taking any chances."

FISK heard the elevator door in the hall open and shut. It was too natural a sound, even at that hour for the other two to pay attention to it. And they hadn't been listening for it. Fisk had. He knew that Williams, seeing him go up to Emily Martin's apartment, would reason along the lines Swenson had just stated and would come up to protect Emily from him.

Fisk raised his voice. "All right, kill me. But it won't help you. My father's cleared. We know that you two murdered Hazel Griffin. My father's bullet only stunned her. Then when he fled, one of you fired a bullet into her heart. I think it was Emily Martin. She and Hazel were jealous of each other. Hazel was taking you away from Emily. Emily's getting old, a has-been; she realized that she hadn't a chance against the younger and more attractive girl. So she saw her chance. As soon as my father fled, she picked up the gun and shot Hazel. You, Swenson, probably wiped off the prints. Emily probably has something hanging over your head—some sort of blackmail. She forced you to become an accessory."

"You've said your piece," Swenson sneered. "Now go for your gun, Boy Scout. Make a move toward me. Or do I have to shoot you down like this?"

Fisk saw the doorknob turn slowly. It made no sound. But Williams couldn't come in; the lock had snapped shut when Fisk had entered.

Fisk said: "You fool, Swenson! Do you think I came alone? This place is surrounded with police. There are detectives in the hall right now."

Emily Martin emitted a terrified cry and started to moan hysterically. Swenson's face turned ashen.

"No good, Fisk. I've more sense than to fall for a line like that. Here goes."

Swenson's teeth dug into his lower lip. His trigger finger started to tighten.

The gun that roared wasn't in the apartment. Surprise swept over Swenson's face; involuntarily he jerked his head toward the door. A moment later his eyes were back on Fisk, but the interval was all Fisk had needed. He was nearly on Swenson when Swenson squeezed the trigger.

Swenson shot too quickly. The slug whistled over Fisk's head. Swenson threw himself out of the way of the detective's charge and went down on his knees. He twisted, bringing up his gun. By that time Fisk had pulled out his own gun, and two shots roared.

Hot lead crashed into Fisk's right shoulder, spinning him against a table. He groped with his good hand for the edge of the table and steadied himself. Haze clouded his sight, and as from far away he heard Emily Martin screaming and he saw a door fly open and Williams plunge into the room.

Williams checked himself and stared down at the still form of Gordon Swenson. "Nice shooting, Sergeant," he grunted. "I heard you from the hall. All I could think of was to shoot at the lock to scare him."

"Thanks," Allen Fisk muttered.

In a short while Captain Rasmussen arrived with a squad. While Allen Fisk was in the bathroom having his wound dressed by one of the men, he heard Emily Martin blubber; "I shot Hazel Griffin and I made Gordon protect me. I knew he had murdered a man several years ago. It was a jealous quarrel over me when I was—was younger. The man's name was . . ."

FISK didn't bother to listen to more. So it was not only the thought of a twenty-year jail sentence that had made Swenson desperate! He had been sure that once Emily Martin started to talk under grilling, she would also tell about that other murder.

Captain Rasmussen came into the bathroom. He was beaming.

"Nice work," he complimented. "What I want to know, though, is how you figured out who it was?"

"When I started thinking about it, I was sure my father couldn't have fired those two shots," Allen Fisk said. "It didn't make sense. Dad might conceivably have shot the girl during a fit of temporary insanity. But I know my father. He's the kindliest man alive. He would never have killed anybody deliberately. Having shot the girl during the struggle, he would have felt instant remorse. I asked myself: After the girl was on the floor, lying there helplessly, could Dad possibly have sent another slug into her in cold blood? The answer was definitely no—especially as he hadn't enough motive. He wanted the girl alive, not dead. The next question was: Why then had Swenson and Emily Martin lied? And who but one of those two could have fired the shot? The answer was plain."

The captain patted Fisk's good shoulder. "I'm glad it turned out this way," he said.

A couple of hours later Allen Fisk sat in his hotel apartment, waiting. His right arm was in a sling. A bellboy had just brought up a late morning newspaper. The story of Emily Martin's confession and of the death of Gordon Swenson was in blaring headlines.

The door opened softly.

"Come in, Dad," Allen Fisk said.

His father moved slowly across the room. He looked worn, haggard.

"I was an old fool," he muttered huskily. "You saved more than my life."

"Forget it, Dad."

Silently Wilber Fisk gripped his son's left hand. They didn't need words. Each understood.

PALACE OF SIN

By OMAR GWINN

Author of "Bank Night in Hell," etc.

Nothing much happened on Kenton's first night until those gambling den lights went out and a dead man's hand inscribed his destiny in blood!

What they were staring at was a comely blonde, and her dress had been ripped down the front

SATAN IS KING IN THIS SMASHING MANHATTAN MELODRAMA!

THIS palace of sin was *not* blue with smoke. It was air-conditioned and it was black and gold modernistic with the kind of swank for which somebody—meaning the customer—has to pay. The whir of the roulette wheels was subdued, genteel, and the voices of the croupiers suave.

Derek Kenton leaned quietly against a wall behind the roulette wheels and watched. The tux he wore was expensive and he filled it with enough brawn to make his job authoritative if ever the need should arise.

"Better than greasepaint, Kenton?"

"Definitely," Kenton said.

He turned his head casually toward the dark slender suavity of Nino Totelli, who ran this gilded resort. Totelli was amiable in the easy, calculating way of the professional gambler who knows the odds are always to the smart.

"Just remember the rules," Totelli said.

"Sure." Kenton arched eyebrows above matinee-idol eyes of a hazel hue. "Never give the heave-o to anybody until diplomacy's had three strikes, never woo a lady accompanied by a gamblin' man, and never spit on the floor."

"That's it," Totelli said. "You're diplomat, not bouncer."

Totelli strolled away. His hard, polite and amiable black eyes took in the play. Those were eyes that were able to tell by a glance at a customer's face whether he was winning or losing, and how much.

There were few customers here tonight. This private casino was isolated in a small Long Island village. Totelli had a financial arrangement with the mayor and the cops, which was more comfortable than trying to buck the regime in morbid Manhattan. Totelli picked his clientele carefully from among people who could afford to gamble, and gamble out of the peanut category. Totelli ran straight games —at least nobody had ever detected any of his games in the blue—seemingly content with merely the natural margin of percentage which accrues to the man running any gambling device. His physical protection was two-fold— a polite gorilla with a machine-gun in a small glassed-in room near the front entrance. The glass was the one-way kind . . . the gorilla could see you when you came in, but you couldn't see him.

A ND inside there was Derek Kenton, actor, new to the job of diplomat. About all he'd ever have to do would be quiet drunks with kid gloves, maybe occasionally handle something else off-trail.

There were few customers tonight for the reason that there was a biting blizzard wailing outside, driving snow viciously against the windows. A couple of portly dowagers incongruously shooting craps. Three dizzy debs and escorts playing roulette; a couple of elderly men likewise; a young male drunk likewise; a guy playing twenty-one.

The young male drunk had an arrogant face.

"Son of the idle rich," Kenton mused. "To bad about the face. He might do to back John's next."

The thought gave the trend of Derek Kenton's thoughts, and the real reason for his being here on this job. Totelli admired Kenton's acting and, finding him between plays, had offered him this as a fill-in. Kenton had snapped it up. The last play he'd been in was knifed by the critics and folded in a week. The floppo had lowered producer John Stannard's prestige as well as his bankroll. He had another play, and a good one, with the lead for Derek . . . and no backer. They shied away from Stannard now, after two flops in a row.

Derek Kenton had figured it wouldn't do any harm to meet multitudes of plutocrats face to face nightly; never could tell what might come. And it's a primary rule of life: to earn money or to get it otherwise you have to go where money *is* . . .

The young drunk lost again, growled sourly, said to the croupier:

"Bette isn't here tonigh', is she?"

The croupier hesitated a moment, nodded briefly toward the stairs.

Kenton watched him, slightly unsteady on his feet, a cruel expression on his arrogant face as he made his way up the broad circular staircase to the second floor. Up there were the private dining rooms, thoughtfully equipped with divans and low lights. The bar and the kitchen were up there, too, at the south end. The series of private dining rooms were really oversized booths, running to the west of a long corridor.

Kenton watched the two portly dowagers shooting dice on the green baize table. They were shooting forty and fifty bucks at a crack and evidently not doing so well. They looked enough alike to be sisters. The shorter of the two seemed nervous. She patted her face with a silk handkerchief, looked toward the long north windows and fanned her face vigorously with the handkerchief. Then she played another fifty and shot snake-eyes. The table man raked the money in, put it in the bank drawer.

Totelli had gone into his office, toward the front of the building at the west. Kenton strolled over to the roulette wheels.

It was then the lights went out over the place, with great suddenness.

Derek Kenton stiffened, felt instinctively for the black automatic in his shoulder holster. Was this maybe a stickup—with somebody figuring to best a machine-gun by that reliable weapon called darkness? Or was it the storm, merely?

"Be calm, please!" Derek ordered in ringing tones.

"Kenton!" It was Totelli's voice, somewhat sharp.

"Yes?"

"Come here."

Kenton made his way to the voice.

"What is this?"

"Probably the storm blew some wires down," Kenton said.

"It's stormed harder than this before, and no wires went down. Come in here. I have a couple of flashlights. I've buzzed the caretaker by phone, in the basement, to have a look around."

THEY went into the office. Totelli groped around in his desk, muttering, "I'd have brought them out, but I thought perhaps the lights were gone only in here."

A piece of the wall opened quietly into Totelli's office and a voice inquired: "What's the lay, boss?"

"I don't know, Jinx. Keep an eye out the front peephole and if you see anything offside, work the chopper," Totelli said. "Nobody's ever tried to squeeze this joint, and maybe this is the time. Get back to your post. Kenton," Totelli said, turning, "keep your fist on that roscoe. There's sixty Gs in this place, and several wrong guys who can know it."

"I think I can see dim light toward town." Kenton was peering through the small high window which looked out of Totelli's office.

"So do I think so," Totelli said. "We go in."

The gorilla with the machine-gun had faded back through the wall into his Rock of Gibraltar room. Anybody leaving in a car would have to go past his line of vision.

As Kenton opened the door, he heard a dull thud from the direction of the center roulette table. Women were chattering, asking questions; there was an undercurrent of men's voices reassuring them. Somebody struck a match to light a cigarette and some woman screamed and fainted. Then another screamed and fainted.

Totelli and Kenton flashed their lights toward the scene.

"Well, they faint," Totelli said. "I suppose they sue me."

"Maybe they had a reason." Kenton elevated his light. "Look: new kind of stakes for roulette."

Totelli had seen, too, by then, and he didn't like it.

"Nice first act curtain," said Kenton.

"It's a whole set of curtains," Totelli said tonelessly, "for the joint and maybe for me."

Well, it was the arrogant-faced young rich guy who looked to Kenton like the spawn of plutocracy. What puzzled Kenton was how he'd gotten there in the middle of that roulette wheel with a paring-knife imbedded in his shirt front.

Kenton and Totelli moved closer and the young guy didn't look any prettier close up. There was an amazed, staring expression on his face, in his eyes, very wide in death. His shirtfront had red pleats where they'd been white before. He didn't have much poise; his legs were sprawled out at angles, his arms limp over the sides. The roulette wheel would require repairs.

The knife had penetrated something else before it had penetrated the young guy's heart. Totelli and Kenton stared.

"The jack of spades," Totelli said.

"Brands his character, perhaps," suggested Kenton. "A knave, with the spade to dig his grave."

"Oh, god, this is awful!" one of the debs wailed. "What a mess! What a mess to get into. Nino, let us out of here. We don't want to be smeared all over the tabloids. Father'll raise hell if he ever learns I was here."

"Take it easy, baby," Totelli said. "There's other things to think about."

There was indeed. A burst of machine-gun fire from the front of the place, for example. It came in fast staccato, and ceased abruptly.

"You stay here!" Totelli ordered Kenton. Totelli glided toward the lookout room.

Kenton looked at the floor. The shortest of the two fat dowagers and one of the debs had swooned, and their respective companions were attempting to revive them.

B UT Kenton's head was in the hook of a question mark: how had this young drunk wound up dead sprawled over the roulette wheel? Had somebody knifed him and thrown him there?

Incredible. He hadn't even been in the room when the lights had gone out. How had he come downstairs, got knifed and up there in that short space of time? It *was* incredible.

"Call a policeman!" the jittery deb yelped.

"What goes on! What's all the shootin' for?" Somebody yelled from upstairs.

"It was just practice," Totelli said calmly from the darkness near the door of his office. "And there'll be no calling of policemen until we discover what this is about."

Kenton elevated his eyebrows, and his finely chiseled matinee idol features were deceptively bland in the dark. He wished he knew more about the ghostly arts—the things that could put a man incredibly dead upon a roulette wheel with the jack of spades spitted on the knife.

Some female yelled from upstairs then.

"Kenton," Totelli called, "go up. Please maintain your composure, my friends. I am sure the lights will be on again shortly. My men are searching for the cause."

Kenton went upstairs at a high gallop, flashlight making a broad and eerie trail for him. He was still wondering what that machine-gun fire had meant down front. Totelli hadn't told anybody, and wouldn't, until it suited his fancy.

He got to the head of the stairs, gazed down the corridor, saw four people staring down at the floor, aided by the glow of a cigarette lighter.

What they were staring at was a comely blonde, and she was unconscious. She manifestly had nice gams and her black evening dress had apparently been ripped down the front.

Gazing down at her were: a waiter

in a white jacket, a tall brunette who seemed to combine the best attributes of Garbo and Dietrich, a sturdy young man who had a ruddy outdoors look about him, and a horse-faced old guy who wore expensive rocks on his fingers.

"Get some smelling salts, get a doctor!" the old guy husked, blinking down at her. "My Pamela!"

"Get out of the way, first, please," Derek Kenton said, and meditated: so this is the way they break; this, my first night on the job, shapes to be my last.

They looked around at him, and the old guy and the waiter stepped aside while Kenton stood there for a moment gazing at the blonde.

"A little whisky might do it," Kenton said. "Waiter, go get a cold towel, some smelling salts, and any other restoratives you have." Kenton stooped, picked the blonde up and asked: "Which booth?"

The old gent with the horse face pointed to the nearest one. Kenton kicked the door inward, strode in with his burden. She was a nice armful and it recalled rehearsals to him, those long weeks of rehearsal in that last play, when he'd carried an unconscious girl like this. Nostalgically, he pinched the blonde and she elevated her hip with a slight jerk. Kenton placed her on the deep leather divan and turned to the old horseface:

"Are you her escort?"

"Yes. M'name's J-Joseph McGilchrist."

Joseph McGilchrist seemed quite drunk.

"What happened?" Kenton asked him.

"I—I don' know." He slumped woozily into a chair. "Lights went out, an' I kin'a dozed . . ."

"Well, sit right there. I'm the producer on this floor and the rest of you are supers, by authority of this." Kenton waggled the automatic.

HE WENT out. The outdoors young man with the ruddy innocent glow of health was there talking in low tones to the tall and comely brunette. They broke off hurriedly and looked at Kenton.

"What's your names?"

"What's it to you?" the outdoors asked in a Western drawl.

"*I* can get tough, too," Kenton said.

"I just wanted to see if you could," the Westerner drawled. "I'm Tod Hawkins, Oklahoma, and this is my cousin, Bette Sloan, who's from New York, Bar Harbor and similar snooty places. Want our fingerprints?"

"So you *know* already there's been a murder?" Kenton jutted his handsome profile forward. "How would you know that, being up here all the time?"

"I heard what sounded like machinegun spit down front a spell ago, so there ought to be somebody dead, inasmuch as this place is run by sinister people," Hawkins answered easily, maybe too easily.

"Yes? Where were you when the lights went out?"

Hawkins flushed a deeper color of red. "I was in the gentlemen's lounge, adjusting my tie, and things."

"And *you?*"

"I was in our private dining-room, toying with a liqueur," the girl Bette said in a low, cultivated tone. She was an attractive creature, all right. So attractive, Kenton wondered why she was here with a cousin when there'd be plenty other guys who would have a non-family interest.

"What're you doing here?"

"What do you suppose?" she asked coolly. "Toddie inherited a piece of an oil well and came to the big town to see the family and to celebrate. I brought him out here a few nights ago, and he lost. He came back tonight to try to recuperate. We came up here for dinner first. Anything criminal attached to that? And are you of the police, by the way?"

"I'm the private police," Kenton said. "Please go into your dining-room and remain there until further notice."

She curtsied mockingly and the Westerner bowed slightly from the waist.

"Wait a minute," Kenton interposed. "What went on here?"

"I was sipping a drink, the lights went out and I decided to wait it out.

Then presently, I heard the sound of feet running in the hall out here, a moan and a thud, and I looked out."

"Same here," said Hawkins, "only I was in the — the gentlemen's lounge, which is the Eastern term for—"

"Never mind that. What then?"

"When I came out, Bette was striking a match and—"

"Where was the blonde's escort?"

"He came to the door, woozy, when I shrieked, seeing the blonde lying there unconscious," Bette said.

"Hammm. Well, go back into your dining-room, please, and stay there."

They went. The waiter was hurrying up the corridor with various restoratives. He was a dark, thin-faced, impassive sort of waiter; eyes a little close set, perhaps, but distinctly noncommittal. He had a flashlight.

"I wonder what can have happened to the lights, sir?"

"We can both wonder. Meanwhile, the blonde," Kenton said.

THE blonde was still limp on the divan, the old rounder still slumped down in his chair staring woozily at the floor. The waiter set to work with ice cubes, smelling salts and whisky.

Presently the blonde opened her eyes weakly and moaned.

"What— —"

"Take it easy," Kenton suggested. He waited patiently, though inwardly impatient to get back downstairs.

The blonde sat up weakly after a time, blinked slowly, felt of the back of her head.

"What happened?" Kenton asked.

"I—I don't know," she whispered, shaking her head slowly. "The lights went out, and stayed out, and I stepped out the door to call the waiter to see what was wrong. Suddenly someone— it felt like a man—bumped into me. Then something hit me on the back of the head, and the man ran on past, and I went out like the lights."

"Hmmm." Kenton eyed her aged escort. There was a pint bottle of brandy nearly empty and some liqueur bottles, too. Kenton frowned. The problem still was: how did that dead guy get on that roulette table? "Stay here," he ordered them and went down.

Totelli and the three croupiers were standing by the roulette table, gazing impassively at the corpse. The debs, the dowagers and the other men customers were sitting in chairs nearby.

Kenton flashed his light up toward the rather high carved oak ceiling. Nothing there, except a chandelier a rod off-center from the roulette table.

"How," Kenton said, "do you suppose he got here?"

Totelli arched his eyebrows imperceptibly ceilingward. "He fell," Totelli said. "I wasn't out here. But he fell."

"Fell from where?"

"From the ceiling."

"How could—"

"Through the ceiling, then," Totelli said. "He fell through it. When I first started this place, Jinx and his chopper were up there," he elevated his eyebrows again, "with peepholes and a trapdoor to keep things in control in case banditti came in to try a win the easy way. I changed all that when I heard about the one-way glass. Jinx has his room front now, so if banditti come, they take and they go out, but they drive their cars past Jinx and he gives them the business with no one getting hurt. It is a much better way than the previous. But the trapdoor is there still, above, and James Morgell II is now down here dead and costing me a fortune."

"Is he of *the* Morgells?"

"Yes, a scabrous bark off the family tree. He gambled, he drank, he was of little utility in this world, save perhaps to me. He lost frequently, and sometimes heavily."

"Hmmm." Kenton ran a slow hand through his hair. Nobody had come running down those stairs when the lights had gone out, because there was no additional human here ... aside from the corpse, who had come the fast way. The murderer, then, was definitely upstairs. Perhaps had made a run at the stairs past the conked blonde, thought better of it and gone back. "What about the lights?"

"I phoned to a friend in the village. The lights there are all on, as I suspected," said Totelli. "These were put out for a purpose. But they were not put out by any inside switch or control. My handymen examined them thoroughly. The answer then—they were crimped from the outside. My men have gone to see."

"What was Jinx doing with the machine-gun?"

"H E thought he saw a car leaving, just as he returned to his post and looked out, after talking with us in my office. He isn't certain. The visibility is low through the snow. He shot, he went out onto the porch. He saw car tracks that looked very fresh."

"So what now?"

"So ruin now," Totelli said. "This closes my place, costs me money, inconveniences patrons who will tell their friends to avoid Totelli, even if he starts anew when this has gone the way of all things."

"You're sure about that, eh?" Kenton asked, a light shining bright inside him. "What would it be worth to you to find yourself mistaken, on the profit side?"

"It would be worth considerable," Totelli said, looking at him. "But there is no way out for me."

"If I found one for you, would it be worth the cost of backing a socko play, from which you'll get your money back double?"

"Show me," Totelli said.

"I'm on the way," Kenton told him, and walked forward for another look at the corpse.

Well, fingerprints were out—there probably wouldn't be any, anyway. Find the motive. Find the proof. He walked over to the customers, who were sitting around staring silently. The fainted deb and dowager had been brought around, and were sitting back limply in easy chairs.

"For your own protection," Kenton began, "I ask you not to make a break for a phone, any of you. I'm sure none of you wish to be involved in scandal, least of all suspected of murder, with your pictures in the tabloids. You all come from genteel families, I am sure, and have no wish to become involved in this sort of thing. The police are best forgotten for the time being. As a matter of fact, anyone attempting to call them may well be strongly suspected of being the murderer—attempting to show undue morality to cover his crime. You are at liberty to wander about on this floor. No one else shall enter tonight. You are at liberty to eat or drink as you wish, at no expense to you. And we shall appreciate your co-opera—"

Kenton broke off. The lights suddenly had come back on. The lights were low, soft, but their sudden reappearance caused startled looks to come over various faces. Totelli merely raised his eyebrows and lit a cigarette.

The caretaker came in presently and announced that the feeder line had been cut outside the house, toward the rear. Luckily, the live end had been protected by the eaves. He'd spliced the wire together, using insulated gloves and rubber boots.

"That's splendid," Totelli said. "Now we turn most of them off again. You, Jacques," he told a croupier, "go to the front door and remain. If any other customers come—which is improbable in this weather—tell them we are not open."

Jacques went. So did Kenton.

He went back upstairs. The room that contained the trapdoor was now a sort of supplementary serving-room or auxiliary bar for the waiters to use when business was heavy. Its door was directly opposite the dining room occupied by the statuesque brunette Bette and her Western cousin. The dining room occupied by the blonde and the old guy was nearer the stairs.

Kenton went into the auxiliary room. It wasn't very big, nor extensively furnished. There was bar equipment, a portable bar, a few bottles on shelves, a few throw rugs on the floor, a couple of chairs.

THE trapdoor was under one of the throw rugs. It slid back, instead of opening up, was neatly camouflaged. There was one of those wicker-covered wine bottles lying on the floor nearby. He picked it up and glanced at it, and while glancing at it saw a shadow behind him. He said, without looking around:

"Bette, was James Morgell II blackmailing you?"

"Why do you wonder?"

Kenton looked around at the tall brunette. She was standing there in the doorway smoking a long cigarette and regarding him with narrowed eyes.

"I just wondered if you hit him with this bottle and dropped him through the trapdoor with that knife in his ribs decorated with a jack of spades," Kenton stated.

The girl started visibly. "What!—"

"He's dead all right. And just before he came upstairs he asked a croupier if you were up here. James Morgell was looking for you and with an unpleasant light in his eye."

"So he's dead," she said, inhaling deeply and letting the smoke out slowly.

"Yes. And if you did it, I wish to congratulate you for your adroitness. There are no bloodstains. There's a bruise above Morgell's left ear. From that I adduce that he was first conked with this bottle, laid over this trapdoor after it was opened, stabbed and dropped through to eternity."

"And about time, too," the girl muttered.

"You think so, do you?" Kenton asked blandly. "You should be careful about making those statements when under suspicion."

"You can't prove I did it, for the quite good reason that I didn't, if he's really dead," the girl said.

"He really is, and now if you'll return to your cage, I'd like to talk to you and your healthy Western cousin."

Gesturing for her to precede him, Kenton went into their private dining-room.

Hawkins, the healthy Westerner, was sipping brandy and was a trifle truculent, his hair rumpled.

"I don't like the idea your orderin' me around, you collar-ad galoot. What's 's all about? I want go down and play roulette, an' I'm not gonna stay here any more."

"Just as a favor to me, stay another five minutes, pard," Kenton said, looking at the young man closely. There was a slight red stain on Hawkins' otherwise immaculate shirt front. Wine, maybe. They'd had burgundy with the food. The girl sat back, her legs crossed calmly, and watched Kenton through non-committal slitted eyes. She had poise, all right, and she'd disliked the corpse.

"Five minutes," Kenton said, bowing slightly. He went out and paused before the door of the dining-room occupied by the blonde and the aged horse-faced McGilchrist. He opened the door suddenly, went in.

McGilchrist was slumped forward in his chair in a drunken stupor. The blonde was limply holding an ice-pack against her forehead, the back of her head limply back against the wall, pain in her wide blue eyes.

"How long must we stay here?" she asked. "Joe needs reviving and I need a doctor."

"Five minutes or so longer, sweetheart," Kenton said. "Mind if I search Joe?"

"If it'll do any good, go ahead," she told him listlessly.

"Who, by the way, *is* Joe?"

"My husband. Why?"

"Oh." This was news to Kenton. He searched Joe, found nothing of importance—except a couple of blue-diamond back playing cards, the ace and deuce of hearts. Cards from the same kind of deck as that from which the knife-skewered jack of spades had come. The blonde watched him listlessly, with only a trace of curiosity.

"How long have you and this man been married?" Kenton asked.

"A little over a year. And we *are* married," she added with a touch of petulant emphasis.

"I'll take your word for it. Please sit tight."

KENTON went out, frowning, headed for the kitchen and serving bar. There was a cook, a swamper, a bartender, and the upstairs waiter. Because trade was light tonight, only one waiter was on duty up here. There was another, but he had been downstairs throughout the period of the murder. Kenton asked them a few questions.

They had all been in here when the lights had gone out. They could vouch for one another. Well, possibly, one might have slipped out. Jack, the waiter, not busy at that moment—the only one who wasn't busy—might have.

"Was James Morgell II insolent to waiters?" Kenton asked.

The waiter tightened slightly, and said, "He was, as a matter of fact."

"Have you been down stairs?"

"Not since the lights went out," said the waiter. "The other waiter brought us up instructions to remain here, some time ago, together with the information that Mr. Morgell is dead."

"Hmmm." Kenton arched a thoughtful eyebrow. "Mind if I search you?"

"Certainly not. Proceed."

Kenton searched, and the only thing of importance he found was a lone blue-diamond-back four of spades. "Where'd this come from?"

"I don't know, sir." The waiter looked with mild surprise down at the left jacket pocket in which the card had been. "I never saw it before."

"Very well. That's all now." Kenton pocketed the card. "I want you all to stay here until called by me or Totelli."

The actor - turned - detective went downstairs meditating with brow furrowed. He had a strong personal reason for wanting to clear this up fast now. Totelli would be as good as his word—if Kenton saved Totelli from having to close the place or make the tabloids or lose a pile of money—well, Totelli would angel the production of the Kenton-Stannard play.

Derek Kenton was not concerned with the minutiae of morals in this case. As a practical proposition, it wasn't Totelli's fault if one customer scragged another within the precincts; and Totelli was running a straight place; if people lost money here it was their own faults —nobody was forcing them to buck the tiger.

Kenton stopped short at the foot of the stairs, stared at the scene. Totelli and the three croupiers were staring at the open money drawer of the dice table. The drawers of the three roulette tables were open, too. Open— and empty. Totelli kept those drawers well stocked with reserve money, and spare chips. Well, the spare chips were still there, but the spare money wasn't. Kenton observed this as he drew nearer. The other customers were standing around the dice table, too, on the other side of it, and staring.

THAT is, all but the two fat middle-aged dowagers were s t a n d i n g around. Kenton missed them immediately, for the sight of the dice table brought back memories, suddenly now. Memories that pieced together, almost —memory of one of them fanning herself vigorously with a pink silk handkerchief while she looked at the window just a little while before the lights had gone out.

"So I lose twenty-two Gs while the lights are out," Totelli said. "So that's it. On top of the murder."

"See you alone a moment, Totelli?" Kenton asked rapidly.

Totelli turned, looked at him, and stepped back.

"Don't search these people for awhile," Kenton told him. "I have an idea. You search them, you'll run into indignation and trouble, and they'll be sour on you. Give me a couple of minutes."

Totelli looked at him impassively for a moment, just the muscles in his jaw moving and said, "All right. But not too long."

Kenton glanced around, and headed for the ladies' room in a grotto around a corner toward the north end of the long room. He thought very strongly that the two ladies of plumpness would be—

He was wrong about that part. But they were in the little fore-foyer and the shorter of them was talking on the phone while the other stood nervously by. The place was dimly lighted. Kenton pulled his automatic, pointed it at the fat short one who was phoning, barked softly:

"Shut up, *but don't hang up*, lady!"

Kenton strode forward rapidly. The fat gal had dropped the receiver. It dangled there making crackly noises while she stared in petrified agony at Kenton.

The actor-detective picked up the receiver, jabbed the gat into the plump gal's quaking flesh, and listened.

"Tillie! Are you listening? Tillie!" the receiver said in a male voice.

"Say yes, and make him keep talking!" Kenton hissed into Tillie's ear.

"Y-yes, Dick. G-go on!" she quavered, rolling her eyes fearfully down at the gat.

"I was telling you one bullet creased a rib, that's all. It glanced. There's a few holes in the back of the tonneau, but they all missed the gas tank. Why the hell didn't you tell me there was a machine-gunner there? If it hadn't been for the snow and my lights being out—"

"I—I didn't know. Shut up! Wrong number!" Tillie said in quiet hysteria, rattled.

"Tell him goodbye now, honey," Kenton whispered, prodding her with

the gat. "I guess I get the lay now."
The receiver was still sputtering queries and the word "Tillie," but Kenton hung it up, and looked at the two fat gals, who were trembling like gelatin lost in a monsoon on the Indian Ocean. There was a great deal of white in their eyes.

"So it was you cute girls who had the light wire cut, so you could swipe the money in the dark," Kenton said. "And it was your boy friend, escaping in a car after cutting the wires, that Jinx shot at. Sure enough, you didn't know about the machine-gun. I think very few do. It's the only ace up Totelli's sleeve. Give, babies. Who are you and what do you know about the murder?"

"Please, please don't connect us with that terrible murder," Tillie pleaded, tears springing into her eyes. "My sister and I are respectable people, from a good family. My husband is well-to-do. He brought me here once in a party to gamble a little, though he sternly disapproves of excessive indulgence. My life has never been very exciting—that's a fat girl's lot in life—and my husband hasn't been very exciting, either. I liked the thrill of gambling for big stakes."

"LADIES your age usually like a last series of thrills, and I guess gambling was the most exciting fling you could think of," Kenton suggested, smiling faintly. "Next time you wave a pink silk handkerchief in signal to a guy parked outside a window in a snowstorm, don't be so obvious about it. It struck me peculiar at the time, but it didn't click significantly until a minute ago out there, abetted by the sight of the dice table and your absence."

"So that's all there is to it," the bigger sister cut in eagerly. "She got to gambling too high, coming out here every time her husband was away from town on business, and she got to stealing negotiable securities from her husband's strongbox, and selling them and gambling the money away—"

"And it's run into so much these last few months, I became panicky, knew I *had* to get the money back, replace those securities before my husband found they were gone. He'd throw me out into the gutter if he ever found out. I was frantic—"

"Just a minute," Kenton interrupted, his tone cynical; "you mean to tell me you had the nerve to dope out this dangerous scheme and go into it, just the two of you and your stooge?"

"Well, no . . ." Tillie hesitated nervously. "About a week ago somebody sent me a letter. It—"

"Yes? What did it say?"

It said that the writer had definite proof Totelli's games were crooked, that he'd been cheating me of my money. Then the letter went on to suggest this plan, to be carried out the first stormy snowy night. All the papers predicted a blizzard today so my sister and I came out, after arranging with a man we could trust to cut the wires. The letter suggested that my sister and I would never be searched when the money was found missing, because we look so innocent. At least, it suggested we wouldn't be searched closely," Tillie added, blushing.

"Likely enough," Kenton agreed. It was a slick plan.

"The letter was signed, A Friend of Yours, and An Enemy of the Gangster Totelli."

"Have it with you now?"

"No. It was typewritten. Whether by man or woman, I don't know."

Kenton scratched his head. No clue, whether male or female, that letter writer. Or wasn't there? A bright gleam came into his eye, and with it an irrelevantly playful notion.

"My guess," Kenton said, "is that

the letter writer told you to hide the money—here!" He grabbed the neck of her dress suddenly, ripped it completely down the front, while Tillie simply stood gasping and blushing in great mortification.

"Sorry," Kenton apologized easily, plucking packets of greenbacks out of the top of her expansive corset. "There was a reason for this. Totelli never would have searched so thoroughly."

"We—the letter suggested that if he started to search us, I would be searched first, and Tillie, with the money on her, would be very indignant, and could even faint. Then, with me innocent, they'd believe Tillie's indignation was real, and wouldn't search her," the sister said.

"Very slick, very slick indeed," Kenton murmured, a bright glitter in his eyes now.

"Are—are you going to turn us over to the police or to that—that horrible gangster?" Tillie quavered, shrinking from that look in Kenton's eyes.

"L ADIES—" Kenton bowed slightly to each in turn, clicking his heels, "I promise you that if things go as I now think they're going to go, you shall suffer no embarrassment nor prosecution. I believe your story, and it is my staunch opinion that you are simply the dupes in a most adroit murder skein. Just relax, remain in here for a time as if here for the normal purpose, and come out in a minute or two as if nothing unusual had happened. I can readily understand your falling for this plan, as it apparently involved little real risk for you—you knew Totelli would merely have taken the money back if he *had* found it on you—and you were desperate."

Kenton kissed each lightly upon the forehead to reassure them of his integrity and glided out. Rapidly he was turning this night's clues on the tread-mill of his mind examining each separately and then in their relation to each other.

And he was beginning to think he had an answer.

One or two things to arrange and plan. And the corpse to search, just in case. He reappeared unobtrusively, drew Totelli aside. "I'll have your money within ten minutes, the answer, and an out for you. Start a private crap game among these downstairs guests to keep them occupied."

Totelli looked at him, shrugged slightly, smiled faintly, said, "You move with rapidity. How? And why?"

"The cat yearns for the mice," Kenton said, and moved over to the corpse.

Totelli stared after him impassively for a moment and then spoke to the guests, telling them they'd while away an interim shooting dice, open game.

Kenton searched through the pockets of the corpse, found only a memo pad of any interest. One of the items caught his attention: Bette, $400, Monday night.

This was Monday night.

Kenton beckoned to a croupier, whispered to him. The croupier moved away and Kenton gazed thoughtfully at the remains of James Morgell II. There was a small pool of blood in the roulette wheel, and the blood hadn't dried out yet. Kenton gazed at it pensively, and then the croupier turned out the lights for him.

The people shooting craps started to buzz nervously in that undertone. Kenton said: "The lights will return in a few moments. Try impersonating people being calm, please."

A few seconds later the croupier turned the lights back on, and Kenton was away from the corpse, staring thoughtfully up at the ceiling. He nodded briefly, then, to the croupier and to the crapshooters, started upstairs briskly.

The statuesque brunette Bette and the Western Hawkins were still in their dining-room, but Hawkins was glaring at the door belligerently, muttering. Bette was smoking, coolly.

"Hello," she said. "It's you again."

"I don' like your face," Hawkins muttered, glaring.

"Never mind my face," Kenton said. "Bette, did you give Morgell II the $400 you were to hand him tonight?"

She started slightly, her eyes narrowed. "No, I didn't. And now he's dead, I won't have, to the rat."

"Why was he blackmailing you?"

"He wasn't blackmailing me exactly. I got high on a party one night and the crap game got higher. When it ended, Morgell II had my I.O.U. for $12,000. He threatened to take it to my mother if I didn't pay off, and my mother's quite moral about things like that. She doesn't know I like to gamble. I've been paying Morgell off out of my allowance, and by selling my things discreetly. Been paying him here, at intervals. I suspect he has several such sources, since his family kicked him out for stealing from inside."

"You may be right," Kenton said.

"You still think I killed him?" Bette asked.

KENTON smiled blandly. "Wait here one minute. Then I want you both to come downstairs. Many have twisted the tiger's tail . . ."

He bowed to Bette and to the truculent Hawkins, smiled blandly and went out. He stopped in at the McGilchrist's. Old Joe was asleep, his head on his chest, in the chair. The blonde was still leaning back limply, her head against the wall.

"Well, Pamela," Kenton said, regarding her with sympathy. "I'd like to have you come downstairs about one minute from now. I guess you'd better leave your husband here. He doesn't

appear to be in shape to navigate."

She looked at him listlessly, still holding the ice-packed towel to her forehead. "Why do you want me to come?"

"Something interesting. Need you for a witness. In one minute. All right?"

She nodded.

Kenton went downstairs, drew Totelli aside. "Take all these gentle citizens into the front parlor and leave them there awhile, with somebody standing by the door to keep 'em in. Don't ask me why. I'll show you. String along."

"I think I will," Totelli said, looking at him.

With considerable suavity, Totelli and the croupiers herded the crapshooters, who now included the two fat females (looking somewhat jittery), into the front parlor.

Kenton pressed the service button for the upstairs waiter. Downstairs there was now only one croupier, Totelli and Kenton.

Presently the waiter came down. Shortly after, the blonde came, followed by Bette and Hawkins. They all glanced at Kenton sharply, or curiously. Totelli and the croupier remained in the background, arms folded, watching Kenton intently.

Kenton bowed politely, waved his arm in a sweeping gesture to four chairs he'd ranged along in front of him in plain sight of the corpse. They all stared at Morgell II.

"Sit down," Kenton said. "It's been a pleasant evening, and the corpse has had little sympathy. Perhaps he doesn't deserve it. But murder is murder—and in this case it was perhaps a little more than that. I think the motive incidentally was concerned with wrecking this establishment and its proprietor, Nino Totelli, along with it. It has had several unusual and somewhat peculiar angles, and it has been notable for the absence of direct bungling.

"I am by profession an actor. Actors learn to observe when others are acting. In my last play, I picked up a playful little sidelight which has been useful to me this night. We're into the third act now and the curtain's about to descend."

The waiter, the blonde Pamela, the beauteous brunette Bette and the Westerner Hawkins were regarding him with varying degrees of intentness now.

Kenton lounged back against the table with deceptive casualness, his eyes drifting down the four before him. "Funny part is," he stated, rubbing his chin, "I guess all my sleuthing was unnecessary, even if I did piece out the answer . . . because the answer was right on Morgell's stiff shirtfront all the time."

He paused, looked easily at the blonde Pamela McGilchrist.

"Pamela," he said, "I'm not sure *why* you killed James Morgell II—no doubt he was blackmailing you—but I'm quite sure you *did* kill him."

THERE was a moment in which the silence hung with icicles. Then the blonde was somewhat less listless. Her blue eyes flashed, her pale face went a shade paler, but she didn't break.

"You're crazy! I didn't even know he was dead!"

"Well, as a matter of fact, he wasn't —when you dropped him thorugh the trapdoor, sweetheart," Kenton said. "Because he had life enough left to scrawl your guilt on the right side of his stiff shirt front, no doubt as you were shoving him through."

Kenton turned easily, lifted the right side of Morgell's tux coat, which was uppermost. That side of the body was not saturated with blood, as Morgell had been stabbed somewhat to the left side of his heart, and that side had landed down on the roulette wheel.

"See?" Kenton pointed at the right side of the shirt.

There in sprawly but unmistakable letters—scrawled in James Morgell's lifeblood—were the words: PAM DID I... The letter *I* trailed off, as if Morgell had died while trying to write the word IT.

"You see, Pamela—he recognized you in the dark, probably from your gloating last whispered words."

"I *didn't whisp—*"

The blonde sprang up, trembling, a livid spot in each pale cheek, stared at the words.

"He died while trying to finish the message. He knew it was you, Pamela. You say you didn't whisper to him. Well, he recognized you, Pam, somehow. Perhaps the feel of your body. You see, the bottle you hit him with was wicker-covered, Pam. You only wanted to knock him out. But you didn't swing it hard enough and he wasn't knocked out. You wanted to stab him for the personal feel of revenge, and because you wanted that card on the knife as a little personal gesture and because you wanted to slip those cards into your husband's coat pocket and the waiter's to mix things up."

The spots of color grew brighter in the blonde's cheeks.

"But he *was—*"

"But he *wasn't* unconscious, Pamela," Kenton said, "and here's the proof." He pointed to the letters, held up the bloody forefinger of Morgell's left hand. "Here's the finger that wrote the words. It's the print of that finger on the bloody letters, as some expert will attest to some jury, unless you make it easy for yourself by telling us *why*, exactly."

The blonde trembled violently,

looked around her frantically like some wild creature wanting to escape its cage. She whirled savagely on Totelli.

"All right!" she flung out, "and if I had another knife I'd finish you, too, Totelli! If Morgell hadn't lost so much money gambling here, he'd never have gotten the idea of blackmailing me blind!"

"How—blackmailing?"

"I married old McGilchrist for his money. I was salting it out on him—I was going to marry the man I love after I'd got us a stake. But Morgell found I was meeting him, knew what I planned, and clamped down hard on me. He bled me for all I'd saved, all I've been salting away. And he'd have hounded me forever. He wasn't worth the powder to blow him to hell. I'm not sorry I did it. I planned to do it here, to ruin you, Totelli, along with him, because I hate you like a snake, even if I can't kill you now. I've virtually had to drag my husband here, waiting for this chance."

"It was really a good idea—that letter-writing gag and the robbery," Kenton said. "It was a great cover-upper—and the cards from the same deck in your husband's pocket—you'd rather have him suspected, in a showdown, than yourself. But the real reason, I think, was that he and the waiter were the only ones you had a chance to plant the cards on, and you did that before killing Morgell. Tie her up, boys."

THE croupier and Totelli managed to tie her hands and feet after a tussle. Then Kenton drew Totelli aside, spoke to him for a moment. Totelli walked back to the blonde.

"All right, baby, we talk terms now. Here's the lay," Totelli said, looking at her. "I can get you away free maybe, in exchange for not mixing me in this, or having the joint pinched. It's this way: Morgell was drunk. He got you alone upstairs, made a pass at you, threatened you with a knife, and I walked in and saw you struggling. In the melee he stabbed himself. We can doctor up a story. I was up there when Morgell fell through the trap door. We can fix that up, too. And the lights, the storm did that. None of the customers will squawk, because none of them know anything—and if they do by any chance, they won't want to get mixed up in the tabloids or in a messy trial. None of them liked Morgell anyway. We can fix up the deal so we both win, baby. How about it?"

Pamela looked at him for awhile.

"I'll think it over," she said, thinking it was better than hanging.

"I'm sure your croupiers are trustworthy, and the waiter—and as for Bette Sloan, I *know* she is, and her Western cousin will be, too, if she tells him to." Kenton looked at Bette significantly.

Bette nodded silently.

"All right, then." And Kenton added: "So now it's settled, I'll break down and confess that *I* guided Morgell's finger as it wrote those words on his shirt, my good companions. The croupier turned the lights out a bit ago, and I did it then."

They stared at him.

"I knew it was you, Pamela, but I had to break you, this being an unusual case. There were clues scattered around, but I added up the best and they pointed to you. When I first found you lying in the hall and carried you in to the divan, I pinched you. When a gal's really unconscious she doesn't feel a pinch, and certainly she doesn't jerk her hip. Then, a little later, when you were revived, you told about being hit on the *back* of the head and felt of the place. But when I dropped in on you twice later on, the back of your head was against the wall—you were leaning on the place you were supposed to have been hit.

"Then the cards—who had a better chance than you to slip them into your husband's pocket, while he was drunk, and into the waiter's, while he was serving you? And last, the letter you wrote to the fat lady. It sounded like a woman—particularly the suggestion about the bloomers as a place for concealing the money. One more thing—Bette was very frank about the blackmailing. I reasoned if Morgell was blackmailing one, why not two or a dozen—particularly a beautiful young blonde married to an old guy, and the blonde a type who's apt to stray. But how'd you know about the trap door and that Morgell would be upstairs?"

"A FRIEND of mine was the architect who remodeled the place for Totelli," she said. "That how I knew about the trap door. And I didn't know Morgell would be upstairs when the lights went out. I knew he'd be here somewhere, he was here every night gambling *my* money. I knew the lights would be out for a long time, and I could find him in the dark and slip back up here. That's why I left the door open a little and got Joe drunk.

Morgell was coming upstairs when the lights went out. I'd already planned to drop him through the trapdoor *if* he was up here. So what?"

"So okay." Kenton drew Totelli aside, told him: "Hide your gambling apparatus for a few days until this blows over. And here are the twenty-two Gs—about enough to produce that play."

Totelli looked at him. "It's yours, if this plan goes."

"It'll go." Kenton looked dreamy-eyed. "I figure we're fixing this with approximate justice. Pamela's life is messed up enough to give her the punishment she merits for killing a rodent. You're saved—and well, I'm an actor, and an actor can't be too moral with the world's best play waiting to be produced."

"That's so," Totelli said.

"The cops never would have solved it anyway," Kenton added. "So my conscience is elastic. This job took an insider."

"That's so," Totelli said.

Kenton looked at the tip of a cigarette, lit it, inhaled deeply and relaxed. Acting was a splendid profession, all right.

THE END

STATEMENT OF THE OWNERSHIP, MANAGEMENT, CIRCULATION, ETC., REQUIRED BY THE ACTS OF CONGRESS OF AUGUST 24, 1912, AND MARCH 3, 1933

Of Detective Short Stories, Published Bi-Monthly at Chicago, Illinois, for October 1, 1938.

State of New York, } ss.
County of New York }

Before me, a Notary Public in and for the State and county aforesaid, personally appeared Abraham Goodman, who, having been duly sworn according to law, deposes and says that he is the Business Manager of the Detective Short Stories Magazine, and that the following is, to the best of his knowledge and belief, a true statement of the ownership, management (and if a daily paper, the circulation), etc., of the aforesaid publication for the date shown in the above caption, required by the Act of August 24, 1912, as amended by the Act of March 3, 1933, embodied in section 537, Postal Laws and Regulations, printed on the reverse of this form, to wit:

1. That the names and addresses of the publisher, editor, managing editor, and business managers are:

Publisher, Martin Goodman, R.K.O. Bldg., Radio City, New York; Editor, Martin Goodman, R.K.O. Bldg., Radio City, New York; Managing Editor, Martin Goodman, R.K.O. Bldg., Radio City, New York; Business Manager, Abraham Goodman, R.K.O. Bldg., Radio City, New York.

2. That the owner is: (If owned by a corporation, its name and address must be stated and also immediately thereunder the names and addresses of stockholders owning or holding one per cent or more of total amount of stock. If not owned by a corporation, the names and addresses of the individual owners must be given. If owned by a firm, company, or other unincorporated concern, its name and address, as well as those of each individual member, must be given.)

Maavis Publications, Inc., R.K.O. Bldg., Radio City, New York; Martin Goodman, R.K.O. Bldg., Radio City, New York; Jean Davis Goodman, R.K.O. Bldg., Radio City, New York.

3. That the known bondholders, mortgagees, and other security holders owning or holding 1 per cent or more of total amount of bonds, mortgages, or other securities are: (If there are none, so state.) None.

4. That the two paragraphs next above, giving the names of the owners, stockholders, and security holders, if any, contain not only the list of stockholders and security holders as they appear upon the books of the company but also, in cases where the stockholder or security holder appears upon the books of the company as trustee or in any other fiduciary relation, the name of the person or corporation for whom such trustee is acting, is given; also that the said two paragraphs contain statements embracing affiant's full knowledge and belief as to the circumstances and conditions under which stockholders and security holders who do not appear upon the books of the company as trustees, hold stock and securities in a capacity other than that of a bona fide owner; and this affiant has no reason to believe that any other person, association, or corporation has any interest direct or indirect in the said stock, bonds, or other securities than as so stated by him.

5. That the average number of copies of each issue of this publication sold or distributed, through the mails or otherwise, to paid subscribers during the twelve months preceding the date shown above is.......... (This information is required from daily publications only.)

ABRAHAM GOODMAN, Business Manager.

Sworn to and subscribed before me this 23rd day of September, 1938.

MAURICE COYNE.

[SEAL]   (My commission expires March 30, 1940.)

New York Co. Clerk No. 502.

LETTER OF THE LAW

By W. T. BALLARD

Author of "Tiger Kid," etc.

Then he swung the jack-handle—hard

One last crack at the underworld was all Captain Bert Babcock wanted . . .

CAPTAIN BERT BABCOCK sat at the desk in his office at the River Precinct station and glowered at the picture which faced him from the far wall.

The picture was of a stern-visaged man of sixty-five, with level, searching blue eyes which seemed focused on big Bert's scowling face.

Bert lowered his eyes from the picture of Lief Johnson. In the old days they'd called Lief "the Honest Swede." Lief had been mayor then. He'd been more than a mayor.

He'd been the father of Harbor City. From a rowdy, tough waterfront village skirting the docks, Lief had built the town into a bustling city which now boasted a population of over two hundred thousand. Lief Johnson had long been dead, but Harbor City continued to grow.

Every year brought more miles of paved streets, more factories and more neat white houses. Lief had built his city solidly. He had begun by reorganizing the town's shoddy police force.

He had called together the four men who, at that time, had served as Harbor City's guardians of the law, and had made them a speech—short and very much to the point.

He'd said, "We can't expect industry and decent citizens to come here unless we can offer them protection. Right now it's so bad that sailors, landing at the harbor, have to come ashore in groups for safety. Last month alone there were five murders in Harbor City, a hundred and ten holdups and so many fights and street brawls that we have no accurate record.

"Now I'm going to add to the force. I'm going to appoint six new men. I'll give you boys a chance to make good— a chance to stay, but you've got to show me. That's all."

One of the first men appointed by Lief Johnson was young Bert Babcock. Bert was just past twenty-one. His father had been a dock laborer, killed in a street brawl with the Dommer gang.

The Dommers were harbor toughs— five brothers around whom the underworld of Harbor City collected. They had laughed when the word came through that Lief Johnson was going to clean up Harbor City, but their laughter had soon changed.

LIEF'S instructions to Bert Babcock and the other new recruits were simple. "Stop the fighting, the holdups and the killings. You boys all know the harbor and the waterfront much better than I do. Clean up the place. I don't care how you do it so long as you stay within the law and play the game

squarely."

They'd taken him literally. They'd gone out and cleaned up the harbor and kept it clean for almost half a century. True, there had remained a criminal element.

A grandson of one of the Dommers still operated a pool hall on Front Street and everyone knew that his place served as a rallying point for the toughs and sluggers which still hung around the docks. Bert Babcock knew this and it made his old blood boil. He longed to grab his nightstick and wade into the place—to crack a few heads and drag the whole stinking crowd off to the station. But times had changed.

With its growth, Harbor City had developed politics. There was a police commission now, a fire commission, a board of aldermen, a city attorney's office. All of them, it seemed to Bert, banded together to handicap the police. Then too, police methods had changed. Radio cars had replaced the men who for years had worn down the sidewalks of Harbor City with their broad-toed shoes.

Two years ago Bert had been shifted from his uptown precinct to the river ward—the slum of Harbor City. Improvements had somehow passed it by. Half-starved children in ragged clothes played in the rough, ill-lit streets. It was a section of squalor and desolation.

Bert had had a row with the police commission. He'd wanted to walk into Dommer's place with a squad and clean it out. The commission had listened coldly. They'd pointed out that, as far as any law was concerned, Dommer had broken none, that there was nothing on which they could base a raid.

Babcock had burned. He'd gone to the mayor. The mayor was new— little more than a kid. But Babcock had expected to be backed up, for the mayor was Lief Johnson's son—Lief Johnson, Jr.

Babcock remembered well when the kid had been born. He'd watched him grow, had presented him with an honorary police badge on his tenth birthday. Lief Junior had gone away from Harbor City, studied law. He'd returned, been elected City Attorney, then Mayor.

Bert Babcock had celebrated on the day that Lief Junior had been elected. He thought that the old times were returning.

Lief Junior had a son—Lief, Third. Bert had gone to see the baby, had been cordially received, but when he went to the mayor's office after his row with the police commission he received a rude shock.

Lief Junior had said, "Look, Bert. Times have changed since you helped Dad clean up this town. We've got to keep the police within the letter of the law. If we don't, we can't expect the people to obey it."

Bert hid his disappointment and left the office. Two days later his transfer to the River Precinct came through. He needed no one to tell him why. He knew.

HE HAD seen other trouble-makers shipped to the sticks. Out here he wouldn't get in the commission's hair so much, or so often. Well, he decided, he wouldn't bother them again, and he didn't. He did his job quietly, well. In two years he never went uptown unless he was sent for, never saw the mayor. But now he'd been sent for.

He rose, lifted his eyes to the picture again. "They're going to break me, Lief Johnson," he whispered. They couldn't two years ago without preferring charges. Now all they have to do is to shove me out on pension. That's what I get after more than forty years . . . a pension—the right to sit around in my stockinged feet until I die." He put on his uniform cap and strode out into the receiving room of the precinct.

He sensed that the desk sergeant was watching, that all of them were watching him. He did not take a department car for that reason. He didn't want the driver studying his thoughts on the way to town. He got his own coupe, drove across the bridge and up through the business district. He knew every inch of this ground. He'd covered it all on foot—walked the beat for years. He slowed the car, idling along, only half conscious of what he saw. Suddenly he stiffened.

A car was drawn up at the curb before Dommer's pool room. Three men were on the sidewalk arguing. Years of police training told Babcock that something was wrong. When the men lifted something from the rear seat of the car Bert's curiosity was aroused.

He braked the coupe to a stop, and before he thought, swung his burly figure to the ground. He hadn't carried a nightstick for years, but he caught up a large jack-handle from the back of the seat and was better than half way to the pool hall door before he realized what he was doing, then he stopped.

This wasn't his precinct. Young Captain Hawks was in charge. It wasn't his business and, in another half hour, he wouldn't even be on the cops. He started to turn back to his car.

To hell with it, he thought. Let the newcomers—the radio boys—the smart police commission—work out their own problems. As he opened the coupe's door he thought of young Dommer's sneering face. Bert's big jaw hardened, his red-knuckled fingers tightened about the jack-handle.

No matter whose precinct it was he was still a cop. Something screwy was happening in that pool hall . . . that was cops' business—search warrant or no. He swung back, barged through the door so suddenly that they did not know he was coming.

Dommer was just starting into the rear office; no one else, save a pimply-faced kid who was racking pool balls, was in sight.

Dommer's black eyes narrowed to pinpoints. His hand was close to the front of his coat as he stepped forward, his slim body blocking Babcock's path. "What do you want, copper?"

Babcock wasted no words. "Who's in the office?"

Dommer lied. "No one. His hand moved closer to the edge of his coat.

BABCOCK did not wait. He swung the jack-handle. Dommer saw it coming, tried to duck, at the same time tugging at his gun. The jack-handle clipped his skull and he went down with a low moan.

The kid at the table squawked, but Babcock charged the office door. The two men inside had no warning.

He beat them to the floor before they could get their guns clear. Then he saw what he was too busy to see before —a blanket-wrapped bundle.

When he pulled the blanket aside he swore. A fair-haired baby of, perhaps two, was inside. Babcock had seen the baby only twice, but he had stared at Lief Johnson's picture too many years not to recognize his grandson. . . .

He called the squad, learned that the boy had been kidnaped less than half an hour before and turned him over to the sergeant. Then he went on to keep his appointment with the police commission.

At the door he paused a moment, his fingers tight on the knob, then he walked into the long room.

The commission chief nodded and shook hands. "Sorry, Captain. The mayor meant to be here, but word just came that . . . that his son has been kidnaped." He rapped for order.

"I have an announcement to make. Captain Bert Babcock, one of our old-

est officers, is being relieved of his duties in the river precinct and . . ." He broke off as the mayor hurried in.

Lief Johnson's face was white, but he was smiling. "Please, Commissioner. May I?" The commissioner nodded.

The mayor walked to the desk. His voice was controlled. "Gentlemen. Forty years ago Bert Babcock helped my dad clean up this town. Two years ago when, due to the depression, conditions were particularly bad in the river ward, we shifted Bert there. To-night, we are proud of him. He has carried out his difficult assignment well. We are relieving him because we need him more at the city hall. Chief Dodge is resigning and Bert Babcock takes his place. Here, Bert." He extended a black case which Bert took dazedly.

Opening it he saw a gold badge with three words: "Bert Babcock, Chief." The old cop raised his startled eyes.

The mayor was speaking. "As if Babcock hadn't already given this city concrete evidence of his qualifications, tonight my son was kidnaped and Bert recovered him almost before the news was flashed to headquarters."

Bert cleared his throat huskily. "Look, Lief . . . Your Honor, I mean . . . I . . . Well, I almost didn't go in there, see . . . I almost . . ."

The mayor said, "But you did. Why did you?"

Babcock flushed. "I guess it was because I just wanted one more crack at them crooks. I figured . . ." He broke off, embarrassed. There were tears close to his eyes. He shivered to remember how nearly . . . how very nearly . . . he had failed to go into that pool hall. The gold badge winked up at him.

His lips moved. "I'll never fail you."

As if in answer to his unspoken words the mayor said, "We know that you'll not fail us, Bert. You never have and we know you never will."

THE COLOR OF BLOOD

By ALLAN K. ECHOLS
Author of "Cockpit Cowardice," etc.

This female was a top-notch jewel-thief—but she figured murder had only one motive!

I found her in the music room, being very effectively comforted

I DIDN'T even have time to think about the significance of almost bumping Sally Wayne off her feet as I rushed through the rich lobby of the Laverne Apartment Hotel. I was late, after expecting such a call ever since I noticed that Nell Mundin was attracting the speculative eyes of some of my acquaintances.

The colored elevator boy, in answer to my order, said, "They won't let you off on that floor. They done found Mr. Mundin daid, an' the cops is in there."

The truth of which made me sore at the breaks I was getting. If I hadn't been on another job I might have kept this from happening—or I might not have. Anyway, by the time I rode up to the floor above, walked down a flight and nagged the harness bull at the door into letting me in on it things were quieting down. The medical examiner was already gone and the photographic department and fingerprint boys were already packing up their gear and heading back to the pinochle game at the station house.

Sergeant Burleson of the Homicide Squad was what you might call a friendly enemy of mine, or maybe more accurately, a contemptuous friend. I suppose you can't expect any better from the blue-serge suit and derby-hat school of detective.

"Who sent for you?" he barked. He hadn't said a pleasant word since he took off his harness a dozen years ago.

"I just smelled the need for a real detective. Tell me what happened, sweetheart. Did they get it?"

I'm not naturally a wisenheimer, but if you don't talk back to those birds . . . Anyway, he dropped me one of those suspicious looks.

"Get what?"

"Now what would I be interested in that they might have got?"

"Yes, they got it, you sea gull. At least, we can't find it. Maybe you know the answer, since you seemed to be expecting something to happen." Then suddenly he snapped, "Weren't you?"

"Sure! When a dress model marries a man like Mundin there's bound to be jewels, and when Mundin buys jewels he is sure to attract the *elite* of the connoisseurs—"

"Thieves, in my language—"

"—and then of course the jewels are suddenly apt to be missing. But tell me, my man—is Mundin really very dead?"

"Reasonably so," Burleson answered. "His heart didn't hold up so well under the impact of the slug. Must have been weak anyway. It was only a .32. Lady's size gun."

BUT I'd already thought of that— and of bumping into Sally Wayne hurrying out of the lobby as I came in.

"Any chance to see the bereaved?" I asked. "Or have you got her under a doctor's care?"

"You mean she should weep herself sick over inheriting a couple of million? She's in the next apartment, waiting for—just sticking around, in case she's needed. Got a friend looking after her. Do you also want to know how much my bank account is, or if I beat my wife?"

But you can't blame him for being sour. I have knocked off a few things right under his nose. He's all bound up with rules and regulations. I'm not. I work for myself. Gals will strut a lot of expensive glass and weak people will steal it. The insurance companies will want it back with no questions asked. And I will take the reward. Life is like that—all vanity. But we all eat.

So I went out of the regular Mundin apartment and down the hall to the one they'd put her in to get her out of the sight of her tragedy.

Her maid opened the door a crack and I shoved my way in. "I want to see Nell—Mrs. Mundin—"

"She ain't seein'—"

"Yes, she is," I answered, and went on in through the high-priced living room looking for her. I found her in the music room. And being very effectively comforted by a young fellow whose shoulders and neck looked familiar to me.

Nell Mundin was something to look at. Set off like a jewel in the Moreau gowns she modeled, it is no wonder that the aged Mundin had thought that she was worth buying and decorating with the fabulous Omar ruby and a few hundred thousand dollars' worth of its lesser lights to keep it company.

The bereaved heard my discreet cough in the doorway and came up for air, wrapping around her the disarranged negligee which might be described as diaphanous. Interrupting a lady's seance with a good looking youth does something to her complexion and eyes. It did to hers, and her voice as well.

I told her who I was. "And being a kind of floating representative of the company that has it insured—you understand—I'd like to hear the bad news from your own lips. I didn't even bother to ask the law what you'd told them."

She looked at me suspiciously. "You could have learned from them—"

"But I wanted the *truth*," I explained mildly, and watched the red flood her face.

"I have told them the truth," she said with what she was sure was icy dignity. "I came in late to dress to go out. My dear—"

"Your husband—go on."

"My husband was already dressed. I had asked him to send downstairs to the vault for my jewelry, and he had done it. Two clerks brought it up and left, so they told the police. When I came in, the jewelry case was open and my big ruby was gone. They didn't touch the little stuff. It's gone—"

"This is of secondary importance, of course," I interrupted. "But about your husband—"

"Of course," and she looked at me as though I were being ironic or something. "He was lying dead with a bullet in him. All mussed up, like there had been a scuffle—oh, it's too terrible ..."

The young man with the handsome profile comforted her with an arm around her waist, but he hadn't said anything yet.

Nell got control of herself. "And then the police came, and Alfred happened along, and he's been such a help. An old friend—Alfred, this is Mr.

er—"

"We know each other," I answered. "How are you Deering?"

"Glad to see you," he said hastily, then dismissed himself. "I've got to be running along, Nell. If there's anything I can do—"

I watched him go, then Nell got the idea that she should explain. "He's such an old friend—just like a brother. There's nothing serious—"

"There's plenty serious," I told her in a hurry. "You're fluttering around the flame of a murder rap, sister, and that's a shame, with all the dough you've got in sight."

AS I say, I'm not one of those hard-boiled birds, but I do know my way around the middle of New York. My business keeps me in that gray element where the black of the underworld mixes with the lily white shirt fronts of the boys with a good bankroll and a good eye for beauty. Meaning the night spots in the East Fifties.

And furthermore, I'm not entirely unfamiliar with the general pattern on which these professional beauties are cut. Maybe once in a while one will hide her flame under a bushel basket by marrying a poor boy and moving to Jackson Heights, but that's just one of those things like a five-legged calf. Those gals know what beauty is for, and they go either for a big-shot on the black side or a big shot on the white side—or both. Which seemed to be what little Nell was doing.

So—they think fast, and I don't deal with them like I would with my maiden aunt. They play the game because they can take it, and that's why I don't feel bad about passing it out. I was watching Nell pretty closely to see how she was taking this.

And I got a surprise when I saw she seemed surprised. Seemed? I knew she was surprised, and that puzzled me a little, but I didn't apologize.

"Sure, lady. You might play both ends against the middle, but they don't usually do it as crudely as you're doing it."

She got hold of herself, and did pretty well, considering that she couldn't wait till they got her husband's body out of the apartment before she fell into Deering's arms. "I'm sure I don't have to listen to any such insults from you," she said without any melodramatic dignity. "But you might explain yourself."

She was a smart girl and I was glad, because you have to do a lot of fishing for information in my racket, and she wasn't trying to put on too much of an act. "Now you're being sensible," I told her. "It's none of my concern who your boy friend is. I've got one job to do. I'm not the law, and it's not my business to even care who killed your husband. He had it coming, for being fool enough to tangle with people like you. I think you were dumb for getting into this mess when you would have got all his money in a few years anyway. But that's beside the point, too. I'm after one thing. I want that Omar ruby back for the insurance company. What's the price?"

She looked at me blankly, and I was pretty sure then that she meant that blank stare. "What do you mean?" she asked. "Do you think I would steal it from myself? Do you think *I* killed my husband?"

Nothing dramatic, understand. A guilty conscience about the boy friend, but she was puzzled, and so was I.

"Sure. You didn't do it. But how about Deering? If the pair of you haven't set the price, what are we waiting for? These things have to be handled fast."

"You're a fool," she said, and she was thinking fast, but not getting anywhere. Still she knew she had a job

of convincing to do. "It's just like you said; Mundin's money goes to me, so why should I have a hand in it? What makes you think I did?"

That's what puzzled me, too. "All right, sister, here's your setup, if you want to keep on playing dumb. Your lover is Al Deering. Your jewel is gone, your husband killed. Al Deering is a very businesslike jewel thief, a gentleman respected throughout his chosen profession. That little set of circumstances is not my business, but it might look a little gray to the police, nessy paw?"

HER face drained as white as it could under the circumstances, and she sat down limply on the chaise lounge which had also been convenient earlier. She was looking through me dumbly, and then I got the idea that maybe she really didn't know all there was to know about her boy friend. As I say, she wasn't dumb, and now she was seeing a mice in Deering's lovemaking.

"He's not," she said, trying to convince herself. "He couldn't be—"

"Sorry," I told her. "But anyway, tell him I'm ready to do business, with the usual no questions asked. He'll be asking you about that angle when he comes back. I'll drop in later to see how things are going. And don't worry —as I said, I'm only interested in that great big beautiful drop of frozen blood—the Omar. And I'm ready to pay."

When I left her she was still sitting there and didn't know I was going. She was pretty scared—and I was pretty puzzled. In my line, you're not bound by rules of evidence. There's only one rule—get the stone back for the insurance company, or go hungry. And I've got an appetite. I'd planted a few seeds, but they had sprouted some fruit that I couldn't quite recognize.

I'd been in there about an hour, so I figured that I might get a break down stairs by now. Maybe Sally Wayne was back. She may have been just going on an errand when I bumped into her in the lobby.

When I rang her bell I got a break —and a slight surprise. She let me into her apartment, and there in her living room was a nice pile of luggage.

"Leaving us?" I asked with a lot more casualness than I felt.

She didn't make any wisecrack about my uncanny deductive ability, and I liked her for that.

"You knew I'd be leaving," she answered with a touch of weariness, and I was glad she gave me credit for being able to put things together. "Just as I knew you'd drop in for a little talk. Well, sit down and let's get it over. I don't like to miss trains."

I always did like that girl, and I might as well tell you why right now. I met her in a business way, long ago, and she was so different from anybody I ever ran into in this racket, and incidentally so smart, that I couldn't help admiring her. She was a gentleman, in a way, if you know what I mean. She may have been thirty-five. She had a dignified youthful face that was somehow made more youthful looking by the gray mist that was forming in her black hair. And she had the youthful figure and graceful carriage of an athlete. And deep eyes that you could never read; she always kept her thoughts hidden behind thin veils of cynical amusement. There was mystery and depth to this woman. What strange quirk had led her into this racket? She should have been the mistress of a great country house. . . . Those deep, gravely-amused eyes hid a tragic something buried too deep for me to ever penetrate. This queer woman was a lady . . . she knew all the answers, but she was a lady, if

that makes sense to you.

And I liked her. In this racket you get to know the folks on both sides of the fence, and you meet such interesting people, as somebody said once for a laugh.

She poured me a drink with her own hands; she knew what I drank because I'd visited her more than once in the course of business. She handed it to me and said, "It's getting so hot, I thought I'd go to the mountains."

I TOOK my drink. "It's getting hotter than you realize—unless you know something you're willing to tell for a change. The way things shape up there's going to be a real storm around here."

"Don't I know it? But what makes you think it will strike me? Did you ever hear of me killing a man?"

"Don't you still have a .32 Smith & Wesson in that airplane bag there, the second from the end?"

"Why *Mister* Classen!"

"He was shot with a .32."

"Shooting people!" she exclaimed. "Did you ever hear of a decent, self-respecting person who amounted to anything in the profession going around shooting people? I tell you, the profession is being ruined by thugs, common thugs, getting into it. The profession is going to the dogs—and I'm getting out."

"If it isn't too late," I reminded her.

She underwent a change. "Yes," she said, and there was real weariness in her voice. It was seldom that she took off her mask, and I was surprised.

She stood leaning against the white Louis XIV mantel, an outwardly poised woman while some great turmoil was going on inside her. She looked at me curiously once or twice, drained her drink, lit a cigarette slowly, and then looked at me for a long moment. I knew there was something coming, and I felt excited. It was like expecting a chance to overhear something that was a dark secret, and you knew you had no business hearing it. It was something like catching somebody at a disadvantage and getting a forbidden look into their souls. It makes you feel uncomfortable.

Suddenly she said, "Classen, in all the years you've been playing this game across the fence from me, you've been a pretty square person. I've met practically nobody but rats—yes, on both sides of the fence. That's why I've played alone."

I didn't try to thank her, but it seemed strange that here I was, a private detective, being glad a woman crook thought I was a regular fellow. What could I say? I was here on business just the same. That's the way things go.

"I've reached the point where I've had enough," she went on, now decided to talk, and seeming eager to get it off her mind. "You've never heard me rat on anybody, and you've at least given me credit for enough sense to get along, so you haven't bothered to ask me too much. So I'm not waiting to fence around with you. I'm in trouble, and I want to wash up and get out—if as you say, it's not too late."

"I'd be glad to help you," I told her. "You know my setup, of course."

"Yes. You're the only dick in this jewel racket that any of the other thieves will do business with. Anyway, I wasn't asking you for help. It's just straight business as usual."

As a matter of fact, I was a little sorry. I'd have been glad to help her, and I wasn't lying when I told her so. As I said, this woman had something— somewhere.

"You know the setup," I told her. "The National's carrying a hundred thousand dollars coverage on that bauble. They're offering thirty through me, with the usual no questions asked.

And offering five publicly. I won't bargain with you, Sally. Half is the top I'll give, and I'll give it to you without any argument if you can get the trinket for me."

She took her hand out of her jacket pocket and threw that quarter of a million dollar ruby squarely into my lap!

I just sat there and stared at it and couldn't breathe for a minute. I was trembling inside like an exhausted runner. It wasn't just that I had my hands on that gem which meant fifteen grand to me for just knowing the right people on both sides of the fence.

IT was the sickening realization of what this meant. I just sat and stared at that thing in my lap, shining red, the color of blood. Murder went with this jewel.

I must have been staring at her for a long time before she broke into my thoughts.

"I know," she said. "That's what I meant when I said I was in trouble. But, Classen, I tell you, I didn't kill that old man."

I was on my feet now, with the trinket in my pocket. And before I could get my mind collected I found myself pacing the room, swinging the thing around my finger by its chain. I tell you, I've been in this racket a long time, and I never did have my feelings parked on my coat sleeve. But here was something that was getting under my skin.

"Yes," I finally told her. "You're in trouble."

"I tell you I didn't do it, Classen."

"All right, I believe you. In spite of your pistol." I pitched the jewel up in the air, caught it and shoved it into my pocket. "My business is finished. I'll get the money for you tomorrow. Now that that's over, we're friends. Want to tell me what happened?"

She sank into the chair and rubbed her forehead as though she had a headache. "God, if I could only tell somebody. Here's what happened. I was after that trinket, just like the others. Deering, the punk, and two or three more that you've certainly seen hovering around like I did, just as soon as the news got out that Mundin had bought the Omar for that girl. Each of us worked in his own way to get it, of course. Deering made a play for the girl. I went after the old man, and I guessed right. The old buzzard was hollow inside."

"What do you mean?"

"Cheap. He gave the girl the ruby, but it cost him more than he wanted to put out on her. An old man like Mundin wasn't fooled by her. But he wanted to make a show. He bought the jewel, had it insured, and when I got to him, he was willing to cooperate to have it stolen. He didn't pay the reported quarter of a million for it. He paid a hundred thousand—and that's what it was insured for. So, tonight, when his little Nell was out to the hairdresser and the jewels came up, he let me know and I just came up and took them. The maid was supposed to take the rap. I took the jewel when he handed it to me, and I came away again, and it was as simple as all that. And when I walked out with it, the old bigshot was alive and quite satisfied with himself."

"And in half an hour he was dead," I said. "Where were you going when I bumped into you downstairs?"

"I was going out to drop it in the mailbox, addressed—you know. But I saw the homicide squad, and I had a hunch something had happened. I didn't even want to mail it to myself. I wanted to get rid of it completely. And get out of such business. It's no profession for a lady when killers get into it."

That last line was a sign she was dropping back into that cynical attitude,

and I wanted to halt it.

"Listen," I said sharply. "That's not the whole story. You didn't ditch it altogether. You wanted this reward money, and you must have needed it pretty bad, to do business with me. You know you're sticking your neck out on this murder business, don't you? The police couldn't be convinced in a million years that the robbery and murder were separate crimes."

"I know it," she said. "But I don't care. If I can get out of this I'll never be in any more trouble. If I can't—I won't either."

I saw what she meant. She was through—one way or another. What terrible thing it was eating at her soul I didn't know—but this woman was suffering past all endurance.

I TRIED in a feeble way to say something, but what can you say? "Don't get any ideas about things like that. What's it all about?"

"I can't go on like this," she said. "Classen, you know I'm not like the rest of those thieves. I don't belong in this element. I hid in it—to keep from disgracing my family. This thievery— I've stolen a lot of jewelry, Classen, and I've been battling with you for a long time. And with the police. But it's not a game, Classen like it is with the rest of them. It's a disease, just like a person who is otherwise normal having a horrible phobia against cats—or some kind of queer compulsion. There's not a criminal idea or thought about me otherwise, except this terrible urge to steal jewels. I hate it myself, and I hate what I have to do afterwards to cover up the act."

Now that she had started, she was pouring out her story with an intensity that was pitiful, and I listened like a confessor.

"When I was young, instead of treating me as being sick in my mind, I was thrown into an asylum. I escaped, but my family felt they were disgraced, and I felt that I was doomed. But now I know better, Classen. I've just learned that they can cure my disease—klepto-mania. I can go to doctors—to psycho-analysts—and get cured, just as any other sick person can. Classen, I know now that I'm not a criminal. I've been sick. But the law hasn't reached that knowledge yet. They'd still throw me in prison. Classen, I want to get well. That's why I want this money. And if I don't—" Her voice trailed off, and for the first time I saw this strange woman break into tears. She wept softly into her handkerchief, and—well, I may put on a hardboiled front, but . . .

Here was a spot for me. My work was done. My money was sure, and one way I kept my business going was to keep out of trouble. Murder wasn't my business. I had the jewel. I was through. . . .

Then I knew I wasn't through at all. I could return the jewel, but—the cops still thought the murder and robbery were one. Wherever I got the jewel, old Sergeant Burleson — my friend — was sure to want to look for the murderer. And my friend had a way with him. . . .

I took her under the chin and lifted her head. "On your feet, girl," I told her. "Get those bags unpacked, and ditch that gun if you've still got it. Get into a negligee and take a sleeping tab-let. You don't know a thing, and never did. I may drop in on you later if I hear anything. And plan to go up to the Academy of Medicine tomorrow and get a list of the names of some good analysts. Be seeing you."

"You know who killed him?"

"Yes, and so do you, but you still wouldn't rat, even to save your own neck. But knowing doesn't do us a bit of good. Not an ounce. We don't have to have jury evidence, but the cops do. They've got a case against you, but they haven't got a case against Al Deering."

"I know it."

"You and I know what happened. Nell gave him a key. She was just dumb enough to carry on an affair with Deering and not figure him to be any more than a gig. That boy was smart, and I figure that he wouldn't have shot unless old Mundin caught him in the act of shaking down the place. That's a close enough bet for my purpose, but it won't convince the cops, because he didn't get the stone and you did. And you can't prove a word of your story with Mundin dead."

"What's the use?" she said hope-lessly. "I might just as well have killed him myself."

"Wait till I come back," I said, and made her promise.

I DUCKED downstairs to the lobby and made two phone calls. First, I called old Burleson. "Do me a favor and maybe I'll have one for you, if you can keep from asking questions."

"What are you messing in now?" he asked.

"There you go. Would you be kind enough to have one of your better-dressed men lounge around the lobby of the Laverne for a couple of hours. If he sees me, you'll have something. If he doesn't, you won't. Yes or no?"

"What—"

"Yes or no?"

"What—

I hung up and dialed another num-ber. He'd have a man there, all right.

I got Nell, the beautiful cloak model, on the wire after a battle with her maid. From ten floors below her, in the hotel lobby, I told her:

"I'm sorry about this afternoon. I still say your boy friend's a crook, but he didn't steal the ruby. *It never was taken out of the apartment.*"

"What?"

"It was hidden there by the person

who took it because it was too hot to keep. I'm coming up there, as fast as I can from downtown. I'll be there in about an hour, and I'll find it for you. In the meantime, don't you go near that apartment—unless you want to be mixed up in murder. Do you understand?"

She did, very weakly, but she did, and I knew a tractor couldn't have budged her out of the temporary apartment she was cowering in.

Then I shot upstairs in the elevator and let myself into the murder apartment with one of a peculiar group of keys I carry.

I would have bet a lot—in fact, I was gambling a lot—that she was already on the phone telling her boy friend the good news, and apologizing for believing he was trifling with her heart.

I turned on a pencil flashlight and looked around, and then decided on the overstuffed chair as the most inconspicuous, and therefore the most likely place the supposed thief would have hidden the hot necklace in a hurry.

And in the bedroom I hid myself, feeling like a man in a detective story.

I heard the rattle of the key on the hall door, then I saw the wedge of light from the hall as the man let himself into the apartment and closed the door behind him. Then his flashlight went on, and danced around the living room, its yellow eye peering into all the possible places that trinket might be.

Then the flashlight hit the chair and the cushion came up.

I heard his slight whistle as his eyes lit on the jewel, and saw it hanging from his hand in the light of his flash.

Then I jumped him—startled him intentionally, and didn't try to get the drop on him. I wanted him to fight, and fight he did.

Boy, that little gun of his barked like a spiteful hound, and my big Luger roared, making more noise, but not

doing too much damage.

And that's how I drove him out into the hall after a few minutes. In the light, one of his bullets pinked me, and then I let him have it—right through the shoulder.

HE went down just as the elevator door clanged open, and I saw Burleson and one of his men pour out.

I dived for Deering and got my hand on that jewel before the Sergeant beat me to it. Burleson had his police positive out, and he was panting to be in a fight. I handed him the trinket.

"Note carefully, my friend," I told him, "that I recovered the missing jewel on behalf of my company, the insurers, and turned it over to you for evidence."

They had Deering leaning drunkenly against the wall and were frisking him. Burleson pocketed the man's gun, but not before I saw it was a .32.

"And what made you decide to come back and haunt this place?" he asked me.

"Nothing in particular," I told him. "But I read a detective story once where a man got caught by the owner while he was robbing a place, and shot him, and things got so hot that he hid the swag right under the cops nose at the scene of the crime, figuring on coming back and getting it later, when the coast was clear. So, I just dropped around—and here was a fellow—"

"Never mind, my friend, you can tell it on the witness stand."

But I didn't. I told you Deering was a smart guy. He had sense enough not to try to make the cops believe the truth. He traded a confession for a twenty-year sentence, and he wrote it to fit Burleson's theory.

Anyway, Deering has twenty years to figure out why I tricked him into going back and finishing the crime he started. And by that time Sally and I —but never mind that.

A CORPSE RIDES THE BLUE LINE
By BRENT NORTH
Author of "Death of The Striptease Queen," etc.

Davis jerked his head around, his eyes wild, vicious

JIM FRANKEL gazed silently out a window from the rear of the packing plant office. To the south was the long area-way, bordered on either side by the squat concrete buildings devoted to the killing and curing of cattle, hogs and sheep. As private investigator for the Pan-Columbian Indemnity and Insurance Corporation, Jim Frankel had an acute interest in why and how fifteen tons of cured meat had vanished from here in the last month.

"Meat," Jim Frankel mused aloud. "I've seen so much of it in the past two days that vegetarian restaurants are going to have my custom exclusively for a solid six months when this job's done."

"Oh? Well, if you don't like the sight and aroma of defunct animals, why did you let your company send you here?" The girl who asked this question was young, pert, pretty and red-headed. She was busily engaged in checking a long series of figures on a strip from an adding machine, sitting there at a desk.

"It wasn't a question of my letting them send me," Jim said. "It was a question of come or quit."

"You mean come or get canned," Joan, the redhead, corrected.

"That's the hard, but true, way to put it. I ran into an accident on my last job. Got conked and didn't do so well. If I clean this up, I get a raise. If I miss, I still get a raise, but from the end of a boot, right out into the snow, and me ould mither no doubt will starve."

"That's sad. I feel for you."

"You feel for me, but you won't find me, because I'm going to take a look around out there," Frankel said. He, too, had red hair, plus a stocky frame and cynical blue eyes. He started for one of the back doors to enter the rectangle for a stroll between the butcher buildings. He could see the beefy red-faced Ed Davis, the plant's night manager, coming toward the office, accompanied by the sallow thin young guy who was night weigher on live stuff. Frequently trucks came in at night through the rear gates, dumped their loads in the pens and went away.

THE beefy Davis carried a lantern in his hand. There were only two or three dinky red lights in all that rectangle.

It was then that Bert Croydon came in via the front door of the office, breezed in, with that light insolence characteristic of him. Croydon was well-knit, handsome in a berry-brown way, and he was the son of the chief stockholder — and the old man was grooming him for the general manager-

ship of the plant.

"Well, my pet," young Croydon greeted the red-headed girl, "I hope you haven't forgotten we have a night-club date."

"At two a. m., yes," she said with pert crispness, glancing at her wristwatch. "That's an hour and a half yet, and I'm a woiking goil."

"I'm good at handling figures. I'll help," he offered.

"But don't try to handle mine."

Young Croydon chuckled without mirth. "Why don't you give up this night job?"

"Somebody has to check the figures on the day's handle and the system here is to do it at night, as you know quite well, and I can't attend designing school in the afternoon and work here at the same time. Here, get to work." She tossed him a column of penciled numbers.

Jim Frankel smiled wryly. He guessed the boss' son wasn't making any great headway with the pretty employee. Glancing out the window, Frankel saw that the night boss Davis and the sallow weigher were heading back toward the south gate, where a green light flashed notice that a truckload of animals was wanting in for unloading.

Peculiar thing about those 15 tons of cured meat which had vanished. First time it had happened, the gate lock had been found sawed off, and a watchman conked. The second time, there hadn't been a clue. The meat was simply gone, no watchman conked or anything—just eight tons of meat vanished into thin air, and the watchman had seen nothing.

At two a. m. all the night force quit, went home, leaving only the watchmen. One watchman was on until two o'clock, two watchmen were on then until daylight.

The indemnity and insurance company for which Frankel worked was snorting—stuck for nearly $5,000 so far and still no answer to this peculiar sort of stealing. Just how that much meat could disappear without a trace was a nice mystery. Something which Jim Frankel had to dope out, or land in a snowdrift on his ear—a penalty for missing on two assignments in a row.

The night watchman was pulling in one heavy steel gate and the weigher the other, as the burly night boss Davis unlocked it. The truck was a big blue one. It rumbled in through the open gates.

With a casual backward glance at the redheaded girl he'd learned to like so much in these past 48 hours, and at the handsome young Croydon whom he resented somehow, Frankel went down the back steps, strolled down the rectangular open area between the squat buildings. The truck had rolled out of sight into the alleyway which led to the unloading pens to the east of the areaway.

Well, this checked. A Blue Line truck was due in with a load of sheep from neighboring Indiana some time between midnight and two. Frankel was keeping track of all entries and exits.

The plaintive bleat of a sheep, doing a solo not too musically, came from the truck as Frankel approached the corner and started around it. He hated sheep. Ghastly animals. Baaaaaa.

When he rounded the corner the sheep was still bleating from within the closed truck. But in front of the truck, under a spreading arc light, somebody else should have been bleating. Frankel froze, stared.

TWO masked men, both burly, were being quite unsocial. One of them held an automatic on the red-faced beefy Davis, the sallow weigher, Jones, and the stocky middle-aged night watchman, Burkett . . . while the other guy busily bound their wrists and ankles with copper wire and thrust gags into their mouths. All three were lying on the ground. The gagger picked up the sallow Jones, tossed him over into a feed chute, started back for Davis.

Frankel reached for his right coat pocket, for his little automatic, and a voice from the shadows behind him said:

"I wouldn't do that if I was you, chum."

It was the kind of tone that meant what it said. From the corner of his eye, Frankel saw he was a big guy, likewise masked. And Frankel was remembering his last job, when he'd gotten conked and so been jerked from the case for alleged carelessness. Frankel hated to repeat the fiasco, because this time it was curtains for his job—and jobs weren't too easy to find in this private sleuthing racket, especially when a guy had the black brand of him. So Frankel replied:

"You aren't me, though—lug!" and reached up with an arm and back with a foot to tilt the guy over.

It was possibly an heroic gesture in the technical sense, but in the practical sense it was most injudicious, because it didn't work. Something hard clipped Frankel above the right ear and he pitched forward. Through the roman candles he saw the guys in front of the truck lifting Burkett, the night watchman, cracking him alongside the head and throwing him over into the deep boarded up feed bin. That and the white letters on the blue side of the truck. Very strange. The Blue Line was a thoroughly reliable trucking outfit. . . .

Frankel had no way of knowing exactly, but he later estimated it must have been nearly half an hour before he opened his eyes. Everything was dark about him, his head throbbed as if hot coals were jogging each other around and about in there. He wiggled eel-fashion, banged himself noisily against the wooden lift-up doors which extended all along the bottom of the building. Well, he was securely wired hand and foot, and gagged to boot. Fine chance of getting away. And likely Davis and Jones and Burkett were in the same fix. Nothing to do but thresh around and hope that maybe the red-haired girl or young Croydon in the office would wonder eventually where they all were, and come to investigate. That was the hell of it. The night shift was light. Just the girl in the office adding up the past day's figures—a necessity the way this business was run—and Davis and Jones to help unload trucks up until two o'clock. Plus the watchman. That was all.

Frankel threshed around for several minutes, trying to find something hard upon which he might saw a strand of the wrist wire in two. There wasn't anything. And it was plenty dark here on the ground, as well as cold. He desisted presently, his wrists chafed and sore.

It was then he heard somebody else threshing around to the east of him. Inside, behind a lift-up ventilator wooden door, one of the series which extended all along the south end of this building which was devoted to sheep pens.

There was an umphhing sound and presently a big figure climbed awkwardly over the three-feet of rough wood panel which was below the uplifting wooden door. The figure was dim reeling groggily, its hands were tearing at its face.

It was Davis, the night manager. Frankel recognized his voice as he sputtered: "Damn gag tastes like flannel! Who're you there on the ground?"

FRANKEL wiggled around, tried to umff through his gag. Davis found

the switch for the arc light, turned it on, stared down at the detective.

"Damn rats did us up fine. Different way each time," Davis growled, rubbing his chafed and wire-gouged wrists. His red face was heavy with wrath. He was about thirty, had been with this company eight years, Frankel knew.

Davis knelt, set about untwisting the wire from Frankel's wrists, muttering the while: "They threw me into the water trough in there. There's a piece of tin nailed across one end to stop a knothole leak. Tin's heavy and has sharp edges. When I came to I worked the wire and finally broke a couple strands. I ducked when they hit me with the gat, but it put me out long enough at that. Bet my bottom buck they loaded up some meat, unless young Croydon spotted them from the office and did something about it."

His wrists freed, Frankel tore away the bandage which held the gag in his mouth and set to work removing the wire from his ankles.

Davis turned, grim-eyed, and scrutinized the ground where the truck had been parked. Suddenly Davis pointed at the ground and exclaimed:

"Look at that! Blue drops of paint on the ground. I thought that truck smelled funny. Fresh paint. The truck was a phoney Blue Liner, fresh painted. By morning it'll be a different color. There was mud all over the license plates, on purpose of course." The night manager cussed fervidly. "The driver had his hat pulled low over his eyes, and the seat was high. I naturally thought it was a real Blue Liner, as one was due, and still is. And there was some sheep baaing in the back. I guess they brought that along to fool us into opening the gates in case we were suspicious."

"I think there was only one sheep. That was all I heard," Frankel stated.

He looked over across the areaway toward the buildings on the west side, where the cured meat was hung in refrigerators.

"Maybe," Davis said. "Anyway, the other two men and I walked around behind the truck to help unload, and the driver jumped out with a mask on his face and a rod in his hand. And then the other two jumped out of the back of the truck. You know the rest."

Frankel nodded. "I guess we'd better untie the other two, and then go look at the refrigerators. I suspect they took a truckload."

"The Blue Liner tonight was scheduled to take half a ton of hams into Chi," Davis said. "So this phoney truck could have loaded to the roof without the girl in the office or young Croydon being suspicious if they happened to look out the window. Brrrr! That damned water in the trough was cold." A strip down the middle of Davis' coat was wet, as were his shoes, and the night air was brisk.

The night manager and Frankel looked inside under the down-hinged doors and saw the sallow Jones and the middle-aged night-watchman at the bottom of the deep feed bin lying on a pile of bran. They dragged both out.

Jones, the sallow weigher, was conscious, though groggy. The watchman was out. Between them they carried him up to the office for restoratives. The office lights were still on, but nobody was there. Leaving Jones there to care for the watchman, Davis and Frankel went back down to the refrigeration building to check up on the losses. Probably the girl and young Croydon had left early, gone on their date, Frankel reflected. . . .

IT was notably more chilly in the outer part of the refrigeration building. Davis snapped on a light and they headed for the bigger ice-box. Davis

opened the door, stood stiffly, staring in frozen amazement. Frankel took one look and stiffened similarly.

His wrists impaled on two meat hooks, young Bert Croydon hung there, his head lolling forward on his chest and his eyes glassily open in the frozen look of death. The temperature in here was very low.

So low that the nude body of Joan Leeds, hanging from a neighboring hook by her beautiful red hair, seemed faintly blue from the cold. There were reddish marks of fingers about her throat, as if she had been choked. Young Croydon had got his another way: his head was soundly bashed in by some blunt instrument.

Wordlessly, the two men stared for seconds at the horrible scene. Frankel felt a chill course through him that didn't come from the frosted pipes in this big ice-box.

Frankel turned, strode out into the anteroom to the phone, called the nearest precinct station in Chi. He knew the captain.

"Send your three best homis out to the Acme Packing Plant on the run. Murder, kid. This is Frankel."

"How are you, Frankel. Murder, eh. O'Kay, give."

Briefly, Frankel outlined the thing. While phoning, he heard the sound of a truck outside the gates in the rear. He went to the door, saw it was a Blue Liner. It honked for him to open the gates to admit them. Frankel sprinted down, peered through the grating, was satisfied that this was the genuine Blue Liner, with a real load of sheep.

"Sorry. Trouble in here. Stay there awhile!" Frankel shouted. "Explain later!"

He went back into the ice-box. Davis was close to young Croydon, shivering as he examined Croydon's head. Frankel walked up to the girl. Something about her appearance suggested there was a vestige of life left; those red marks on her throat. She'd been choked hard.

"The swine!" Frankel grated, feeling her pulse. "Killed in cold blood. But why? Were the thieves surprised?"

"Likely," Davis grunted. "These two must have noticed something suspicious, come down to see, and one of the guys conked Croydon too hard, saw he was dead, and had to kill the girl too, to shut her up."

"No doubt about it," Jim Frankel said. "I suppose tearing their clothes off was just to give a nice macabre polish to the stunt. Wait a minute! The girl's still alive. Pulse is faint as a feather, but she's still got the breath of life in her."

"My God! I hope so," Davis said hoarsely, staring at her. "We'll take her to a doc." Davis snatched up a butcher knife, hacked at the strands of her red hair which held her on the hook, while Frankel held her body. She dropped into his arms limply.

"We'll have a doctor come here, and meanwhile we'll do all we can to revive her. There's plenty of equipment in that office emergency kit."

"But not enough to bring Burkett around," the thin weigher, Jones, said suddenly behind them. "Better make it two doctors. Burkett's in bad shape. So's my head." He was a very thin-faced guy, with nervous grey eyes, so watery they were in danger of freezing in here. For that matter, so was the strip down the back of Davis' black coat. It was stiff where the water-streak was freezing.

And Frankel's own back was itching from the splinters he'd picked up rubbing against the rough boards when trying to free himself. His head still ached fiendishly. He'd be as glad as anybody to have the ministrations of a doctor.

BETWEEN the three of them, after phoning for a doctor, they carried the girl up, covering her with her own coat, and placed her on a cot near the unconscious watchman.

Davis rolled up his sleeves and set about working briskly and efficiently to bring the girl around. Davis had plenty of experience at first aid. Mishaps were common in this business.

Frankel examined the watchman's head. He had been hit above the ear with the flat of a gat. But being older, he wasn't reviving so rapidly. Feeling of the bruise, Frankel was certain the injury wasn't fatal.

"The boys around Chi are *still* tough, all right," the thin Jones said, his watery blue eyes blinking at the watchman and the girl. "Think no more of a killing than shooting at a tin can. This reminds me of the work of that guy Sclacha, a year or so back. Tore dames' clothes off and choked them to death."

Frankel looked at Jones meditatively for a moment and suggested, "Jones, I'd like you to come back down with me. I want you to watch Bert Croydon's body till the cops come. And we'd better open the gates and let that Blue Line truck in to unload. No use leaving them out there all night. Not much we can do here. The doc and the cops ought to be along any time now."

Jones blinked at him for a moment, his pale face twitching a little. He started to protest, then seemed to change his mind.

"You can hold the fort for a few minutes," Frankel said to Davis, busy administering artificial respiration to the girl, while hot towels steamed over her.

Davis grunted assent, without missing a push.

"Go ahead," Frankel ordered Jones, and the thin, watery-eyed guy went down ahead of him. Half a minute later, Jones was in the ice-box, shivering and gazing after Frankel's receding figure.

Frankel's back was still itching. He was glad it was, now. He moved rapidly, frowning. Into the place where that phoney Blue Liner truck had stopped. Into the unloading pens.

In the flickering light of his matches, Frankel examined the crude splintery watering trough, with its patch of tin. Four seconds sufficed. There was some water in its v-shaped bottom.

Frankel sped over to the refrigerator, called Jones out.

A few seconds later, they crept up the back steps to the rear door of the office. Frankel grabbed Jones' wrist to hold him to silence, and peered in through the door glass.

The sight was not a pleasant one, but it was approximately what Frankel expected.

The burly Ed Davis had his heavy knee on the girl's chest while one of his powerful hands held her nostrils tightly shut and the other hand cut off all possibility for her to breathe through the mouth.

He was suffocating her, putting the finishing touches.

The girl struggled feebly, not fully conscious, although his brisk efforts at resuscitation while Frankel was watching had done more to revive her than he had desired. She was a healthy girl, as evidenced by her recuperative power, by the fact that most of the blue color had left her beautiful body, now uncovered for the most part.

As she struggled weakly, Davis' heavy red face turned to glance furtively out of the rear windows. Frankel had been careful, however, to keep out of the light, and the steps to the rear of the office were in the southeast corner, away from the windows.

FRANKEL had brought Jones back as a witness, and he hoped that the sallow weigher wouldn't grow white feathers if the going got tough. Jones was quaking already.

"You see what he's doing?" Frankel hissed.

"Yes," Jones whispered, turning a shade paler.

The *girl* wasn't turning any paler. She was on the way to turning blue again, and Frankel thanked his personal gods that he'd hurried.

He gripped his automatic firmly, pushed the door open, said:

"Hold it, Davis! I take it your motto is, if at first you don't succeed, give it a second whirl."

Davis jerked his head around hard, and his eyes were suddenly as vicious as they were startled.

And all in the same gesture he dived over the emergency cot, dragging the girl with him. And the cot was standing on its side, a barrier between them and Frankel.

"I've got a knife!" Davis snarled over the cot. "You come a step closer and I'll shove it through her!"

Frankel stopped abruptly in his forward plunge. Ten to one the guy was telling the truth. Cold sweat began to stand out on his forehead. If he could stall Davis for awhile, maybe. . . .

"Next time you bash in the head of a boss' son, do it with the flat of the gat above the ear," Frankel said. "The boys in the truck were professional about it. They knew how to do it without fracturing a skull. That's what made me think they didn't kill Croydon, because the front of his head was whanged with the *butt* of a gun."

"Smart guy, you are," Davis rasped. "Well, I'm going out of here in one piece, unless you want the dame finished up."

"And the next time you pretend you've been lying in a watering trough for half an hour, don't just dip down into it," Frankel continued. "I guess you've heard of cloth osmosis. If you'd been lying in that trough half an hour, struggling to get those wires broken off your wrists, the whole back of your coat would have been wet instead of just that strip a few inches wide. You were thorough and adroit about everything else—even had them wire you and tap you alongside the head—but two little omissions put me on your trail, Davis; added up, they spell the hot squat."

"That's what you think," Davis snarled. "We're makin' a deal. I go out of here alive, with ten minutes head start, or the dame goes to hell, where that cold shoulder she's been putting my way too long will get warmed up."

"What's the deal?" Frankel asked. Beads of perspiration were chilling him all over. Jones was poised silently beside him, staring.

"I carry the dame out front with my knife against her back. I get into my car with her, I drive away. You come after me or send any cops, and I kill her before you or the cops get a shot at me."

"What guarantee do I have that you don't kill her anyway?"

"You got my word."

"I see. And that's worth one Confederate dollar, paper."

"You'll take it, and right now," Davis rasped. "And just remember, one word to the cops or any chase by you and it's curtains for her."

Dimly in the distance, Frankel thought he could hear a sound, a sound he'd been waiting for. He added up the possibilities fast. Davis had the whiphand all right, and if he ever got away in a car with the girl, it would be her end just as certainly as if she died here. But there was still one chance, a long shot.

"All right," Frankel said.

DAVIS arose from behind the cot, the beautiful red-headed Joan draped in front of his body, his left arm holding her in front of him while his right hand held the knife against her bare back. She was semi-conscious again now, moaning feebly. Davis had had time to shut her breath off for less than a minute, and four or five minutes are necessary to kill by suffocation. Davis obviously had figured on having that much time while Frankel and Jones were absent and the watchman was unconscious. That way it would appear that Joan had died in spite of Davis' efforts to resuscitate her.

The burly red-faced night-manager edged toward the front door, a glare of almost maniacal intensity in his piggish eyes.

Frankel's hand was trembling a little from nervousness and tension. He couldn't risk a shot. The only parts of Davis exposed were spots that would require expert shooting and would merely wound him, at best.

Davis lowered his left hand to the doorknob and said:

"I got a rod in the sidepocket of my car, and remember it. Both you monkeys lie down on the floor now and stay there. If I see either one of you coming out this door or looking out the window, I'll let you have it, and the dame, too. Toss me your gat, Frankel."

To impress the detective that he meant business, Davis jabbed the girl slightly with the knife. And that was an error which was on the debit side of his chance to succeed.

Frankel had abandoned hope of the carful of cops appearing in time to be of aid, was on the point of skidding the gun to Davis.

And then the girl, jabbed by the sharp point of that knife, came out of her semi-coma. She trembled violently, opened her eyes, stared for a moment in dazed bewilderment at Davis.

Then she recognized him, and remembered. Her body may have been weak, but the human jaw retains its strength beyond all other parts of the body. Her eyes were suddenly hot with hate and frenzy, and her teeth sunk viciously into Davis' cheek. He wasn't expecting that.

Davis snarled a startled curse, instinctively jerked his head back and sidewise. And at the same moment he drew his right hand back to plunge the knife.

Only a portion of Davis' head was exposed, and Frankel shot fast. A deep red gash appeared along the right side of Davis' head, and as he started the knife on its home trip, Frankel shot again, this time for the right elbow of Davis' arm.

The right arm jerked spasmodically, and the knife clattered to the floor from Davis' useless hand. The girl slumped weakly to the floor.

Davis reeled back through the door, pawing at the blood which was streaming into one eye, cursing like a drunken pirate, reviling Joan, young Croydon and Frankel with a vicious impartiality.

Frankel leaped forward, grabbed him by the shirtfront with his left hand and cracked him over the left ear with the flat of his gat, in the approved professional manner which doesn't fracture the skull.

"Too bad, cull," Frankel murmured. "You shouldn't have jabbed her with that knife. You jabbed yourself right into the hot seat."

Davis lay there in a heap, and he didn't have any answer. . . .

The cops drove in a bit later, and took over. The doctor arrived a couple minutes after them and set about reviving the night watchman and Davis.

DAVIS talked later, but he was alternately surly, dazed, and defiant. He refused to give the identity of his confederates. the meat thieves. Frankel phoned Chicago headquarters, broadcasting a general alarm for cops in three states to stop and check up thoroughly on every truck which carried the Blue Line emblem.

He pieced it together for the cops: that Davis had helped conk the watchman and broken the lock on the gate for the first robbery, that he'd connived also in the second, and had invented this phoney Blue Line truck idea for the third. He hated young Croydon because he was being groomed for the general managership of the plant when Davis had felt he rated it for himself, had even been demoted by the Old Man to this night job. On top of that, he was insanely jealous of Joan, who had spurned all his advances in favor of young Croydon. Davis' love had turned to an insane hate and the stolen meat gave him the money he was losing in salary and was perfect to cover his murder of the girl and young Croydon.

While Frankel, Jones, and the watchman were unconscious, Davis had called Croydon and the girl down to the icebox, had killed Croydon, attempted to harm the girl and then had choked her until she seemed dead. He hadn't choked quite long enough, however, and she was healthy. He'd been hurried, wishing to plant his alibi in the water trough before Frankel awakened.

Joan, when she at last sat up and knew what was responsible for her being alive, planted a gentle kiss on Frankel's brow.

And when he recovered from that, he sent a telegram to the boss of his agency. It read:

I'LL TAKE THAT RAISE, BUT NOT FROM THE END OF YOUR BOOT.

THE END

SATAN IS A HITCH-HIKER

L. A. SIMPSON, farmer, was driving his battered car along the country roads near his native town in Oklahoma. In the front seat with him was his 14-year old son, Louis.

A man at the side of the road held up a stiffened thumb. He was young, only 23, he told the farmer who gave him the lift. There was something likable about the immature smile on the youth's bland countenance.

When he said a cheerful, "Howdy" and grinned, Simpson took him for one of his own people. When he said he was Chester Comer, itinerant oil field worker, on his way to the next town to get another job, Simpson remarked:

"That's a nice name, son. I seem to recollect that it's a good name too in Oklahoma. Nice, respectable folk, the Comers that I knew."

If Simpson had only known what lay in store for him, he would never have stopped his car that day on the Oklahoma road

Simpson and his son were never seen again.

Ray Evans, Shawnee lawyer and man of prominence in the city, liked the affable Comer, too. And so he gave him a ride when the lifted thumb of the hitch-hiker told him that was what he wanted.

For more than a week Evans' family and the police searched for him. Then they found his automobile in a ditch with nothing in it but a bloody sock.

Elizabeth Childers Comer, divorced wife of the hitch-hiker and about to become a mother, was riding with a friend along one of Oklahoma's country roads. The friend gave the young man a hitch. Later, the body of the young wife was found on a lonely roadside with five bullet holes in her head.

His second wife met with a similar fate when she rode with her husband. The partially burned body of a young woman found in a ditch near Edmond was identified as that of Lucille Comer.

When Chester Comer rode through the countryside of Oklahoma, death rode with him. The police say that he murdered everyone who gave him a lift.

But neither for money nor for profit did he kill.

He told the police:

"There is a certain thrill about seeing a man die, more of a thrill than is to be gotten out of the actual act of killing him."

Nothing fazed him, so cruel was the hard-bitten young man who rode through the West, murder in his heart, death often riding by his side.

In his pockets he carried a card which read:

"If I am killed in this car, I have nothing to regret."

For months Comer loomed as the bad man of the Southwest. His very name terrified women and set little children to screaming.

And then it was that the Southwest produced its hero, a hero who suddenly, violently brought to an end the career of the hitch-hiking murderer.

LET Marshal Oscar Morgan, of Blanchard, tell the story.

He says:

"For three days Simpson and his son had been missing. Then one of my men telephoned to me. He said, 'Hey, boss, think I have found that farmer, Simpson, and his kid.' So I put on my holster, stuck a pistol in it, jumped into my automobile.

"When I got to Simpson's car the sight I saw suddenly made my blood run cold. The man in that car was dead, maybe, my man had told me. I

(Continued on Page 111)

MURDER'S A SURE THING
By WYATT BLASSINGAME
Author of "Bullet-Proof Rat Trap," etc.

He tried to make a killing on that last race—and it turned out to be murder!

Out of the darkness the man lunged, a knife in his hand slashing down

LIMITLESS DEAN waited at the top of the ramp, while the judges studied the picture finish of the fourth race. His lean, dark face showed not a trace of emotion; his hands were steady when he lighted a cigaret, but he could feel the muscles still trembling inside him. It wasn't the money. It was just what a good horse race did to him. There wasn't anything in the world like it.

The judges straightened and put down their magnifying glasses—it had been that close. The slot on the tote board swung. And a great heavy noise went up from the crowd, half moan, half cheer.

Dean didn't move. He looked at the number, his mouth set so that you couldn't tell whether the top lip was naturally a little crooked or whether he was smiling, half cynical, half amused. He finished his cigarette, went down the ramp and inside to the ten dollar pay window where for twenty tickets he collected seven hundred and twenty dollars.

He didn't go to the paddock: all the horses looked pretty in the paddock; and anyway, they paid off on speed, not beauty. So he didn't see that Jimmy Aldrich was saddling a big black colt called Lookout, and he didn't notice this on either the program or the racing form. He didn't even know that Jimmy was in New Orleans until he felt the tap on his arm and looked up.

A TALL, thin young man who carried a folded horse blanket over one arm was grinning down at him. "Hello, Limitless!" Jimmy Aldrich said. "Still picking losers?" His cheeks were flushed and his eyes had a kind of misty glitter. He looked very pleased at seeing Limitless Dean.

Dean stood up and shook hands. He had met Jimmy at River Downs several years before when the kid had been just a punk around his father's small stable of platers. Then Jimmy had come down with tuberculosis and been shipped off to a sanitarium. Dean had lent the father money which the old man had repaid before his death, and Dean had taken some interest in the kid. He liked him. Jimmy had been out of the San now for nearly two years, the first one of them spent chiefly on his back. Illness and horses were all he had ever known.

"Got anything in this race?" Jimmy said.

"I was just figuring."

The boy hesitated. He didn't like to tout, but he owed Dean a debt of gratitude, and this was a chance to do a favor. "I got a horse running," he said. "Lookout. He ought to do it."

"Thanks," Dean said. "I'll get down on him." The tote board showed that the odds on Lookout were fifteen to one.

Dean's gaze came back to the boy's flushed cheeks. "How're you getting along, Jimmy?"

The boy grinned. He had a clean, appealing smile. But it wasn't that. Even before he spoke Dean felt the courage, the sheer, terrible gallantry behind that grin. "Oh, I turned up positive again the other day. I got to go back to the San." As if in proof of what he said he coughed, turning his head; but Dean saw the fleck of blood at his lips before he spat into a handkerchief.

"Bad?" Dean asked. "You won't be there long?"

"Couple of years, if I'm lucky. Probably they'll have to take out all the ribs on one side this time. Leave you just half a man." He was still smiling, and it took a gambler's ability to read behind his face and voice. Jimmy knew what the operation meant, maybe death, maybe horrible physical distortion; at the best it left you "Just half a man," able to lead a life of comparative comfort, but no exercise, never again the excitement and work of the back side of the track. No galloping horses in the gray, foggy dawn, no rearing thoroughbred to be saddled in the paddock, to be scrubbed down and cooled off after the race. He knew all that, but it didn't show in his face.

"That's why I'm trying to make a killing on this race," Jimmy said. "I should have left a couple of weeks ago, but I was waiting for my spot." He was talking quietly, so low that no one in the crowd could hear, but at the same time without giving the appearance of whispering. "Lookout's been covered up," he said. "He hasn't raced this year, and he wasn't very hot as a two year old. But he'll carry the mail today for sure—"

"You down on him heavy?" Dean interrupted.

"WITH all I could get. A guy needs a little money in the San. If he's paying his way, he gets a lot of breaks. And I'll need something when I come out. If it's a thoracoplasty I won't be able to do any more real work." He looked down the track to where the horses had turned at the far end of the stretch and were parading back toward the barrier. He lighted a cigarette and his fingers were trembling a little.

"If Lookout comes through I'm set," he said. "I got a hundred on him in the morning line at twelve to one, and another hundred in the mutuals. I can pay off Lookout's feedbill—he's in hock for feed now—and have nearly two grand left over. That'll let me pay my way in the San for a couple of years. And Tom Hendricks will train Lookout along with his horses and give me a split on the purses. Lookout's going to be good this year. I hope."

It occurred to Dean that this, for Jimmy Aldrich, was *the* race. Horsemen don't take a loss as seriously as the layman would expect. There's always another race coming up and they expect to win that, or at least the one after it. But for Jimmy Aldrich this was *the* race. It was this one or none for a long, long time—maybe forever. And he was betting more than money on it. He was trying to be able to pay his own way, trying for the feeling of self respect which this gave a man, even when he lay on his back for long month after month. And he was betting his chief interest in continuing to live, his feeling of possession and of accomplishment in the outside world which owning the horse would give him.

"Get on him, Limitless," Jimmy Aldrich said. "He's good."

"Thanks," Dean said. "Wait for me."

He went down the ramp, noticing that the odds on the horse were still fifteen to one. Jimmy Aldrich's hundred must be practically all the money Lookout was carrying. If Dean bet much he'd cut down the odds. As it was, Jimmy Aldrich stood to take nearly everything in the winning pool.

Dean bought one ten dollar ticket and put it with a batch he'd had left after the second race. Holding them clumped together he went back out to the ramp again.

The horses were going into the gate for the start of the mile and seventy. Lookout was number four. "He's slow starting," Jimmy said. "They may cut him off at the turn. But when he gets around and into the stretch it won't matter."

There was a long wait. The number seven horse kept breaking through. An assistant starter braced in front of him, waving his whip. Then they broke, surging in an even wave toward the stands, the roar of the crowd drowning out the hoof beats. The wave of horses grew ragged.

"He's clear!" Jimmy was shouting. "He's clear!"

The number one horse had gone out on top. A bay from the outside was second, but not far enough out to cut over on the others as they swept into the turn. Lookout was running fourth and still there when they turned into the backstretch.

The metallic voice of the loudspeaker clanged over the crowd. "At the quarter. It's Maisy's Boy by one length. Hopalong second by a half. Yellow Jacket by a head and Lookout running fourth by two."

THROUGH his glasses Dean could see the horse's powerful stride, the way the jockey held him in light restraint as Lookout began to move up. Toward the turn he was running neck and neck for second, still on the rail and saving ground. "Just bring him on!" Jimmy was yelling. "Bring him on, Punk! Bring him home!"

Then it happened, without apparent reason. Lookout began to toss his head. One horse went by him. Another. The jockey was down low talking to him. Lookout's stride broke, caught again. The jockey took to his whip but it wasn't any good. The horse was done. He turned into the stretch fifth and never made a race of it.

Limitless Dean didn't know which horse won. He was watching Lookout come up the stretch, a tired, beaten horse with the jockey holding him in. Jimmy Aldrich was watching too, until he turned toward Dean. His face had bright crimson and white splotches. He said, "I'm sorry, Limitless. I didn't mean to tout you on—on a flop. I thought he could do it." Then he turned and went down the ramp and out on the track where the horses were coming back.

And Limitless Dean felt suddenly very humble. He had gambled all his life. He had lost fortunes without changing that half cynical twist of his mouth. But Jimmy Aldrich had lost more than money, and apologized for touting Dean on the wrong horse.

That night in a bar on Mystery Street Dean saw the youngster again. Jimmy called him over to a booth where he was sitting alone back of a glass of flattening beer. "I hope you didn't drop much," he said.

"Not much." Dean noticed the boy's flushed face, the sheen of his eyes. "Shouldn't you be at home in bed?"

"I got to meet Clancy Bingham here and settle up about my horse. I owe him a feed bill, and more. But I ought to have about a hundred left when he takes Lookout."

"What are you going to do?"

Jimmy Aldrich tried to show that it wasn't of any importance. "Oh they'll take you at the San whether you got money or not. And it really doesn't make much difference. I just wanted to pay my way if I could."

"I'm pretty flush now," Dean said. "I could let you have a couple of grand." That was all the money he had, but money had never meant much to Limitless Dean. He made fortunes gambling and he lost them the same way. It didn't bother him. He could always get money. Among the gambling gentry he had a name for honesty. From any big-time gambling house or gambler, Limitless Dean could get five thousand on the collateral of his promise. But the thing that other gamblers couldn't understand was that frequently he preferred to work for his stake. It freshened him, he said, made him keener. He was a good newspaperman and could generally get a job.

Jimmy Aldrich shook his head. "I couldn't repay," he said. "What I called you for—" he hesitated. "I'm not trying to alibi my horse, Limitless. But he should have won that race. He was sponged."

"Sponged? You mean. . . ?"

"I don't know who did it. He was all right this morning. I looked him over after the race and found them."

"But why'd you suspect? Just because he stopped that way?"

THE boy coughed and turned his head while he spat into a blood-stained handkerchief. "There's been a lot of crooked work around the track this year. A hell of a lot. Always there are guys having their own horses snagged a couple of races, and jockeys' day, and that sort of thing. But this season. . . ."

"What?" Dean asked.

"I don't know. Since they started

this narcotic inspection hardly anybody dopes their horses. You can't even give 'em a pint of liquor without being set down. But there have been some horses doped where the trainer didn't know anything about it. And at least a half dozen sponged."

"Why in devil don't folks do something about it?"

"How? It must be some outsider. Nobody seems to have any idea who."

Dean could feel anger crowding against his brain. It wasn't the thought of crooked gambling that got him. He was used to that. Loaded dice and wired wheels and marked cards were all parts of the trade. But he liked horses, and the idea of physically injuring them to win money burned him. But what he remembered most clearly was Jimmy Aldrich's face, crimson mottled with his disease, as he said, "I'm sorry I touted you on a flop."

"Damn it," Dean said, "there ought to be some way to find who's back of this. If a man were to really try—"

A voice at his elbow said, "So it's Limitless Dean shooting off again. What are you doing, Limitless, explaining why your system didn't work?"

A fat man with red jowls and a broken nose stood at the table's edge. His shoulders were wide, but his stomach was bigger than his chest by eight inches. His clothes were expensive, yet didn't fit. He was fat, and sloppy, and uncouth looking. There were two things about him, however, that belied that look of softness; the little dull eyes under their heavy lids, and his hands which were white and small with a way of moving so fast as to be almost invisible. "Always belly aching," he said to Dean.

Dean looked at him a moment without any expression, then turned back to Jimmy Aldrich. "You said there was something rotten around the track. I've got an idea what it is."

The fat man pushed into the opposite side of the booth and sat down. A small, wizened fellow with the greedy eyes of a pig followed. The little man said, "Hello, Jimmy. This is Mr. Armsted, Harry Armsted."

Jimmy nodded. He was puzzled at Dean's attitude, but he said, "Limitless, meet Clancy Bingham. He's the man getting Lookout off me. And you know Mr. Armsted?"

"Sure I know Limitless," the fat man said. "What's he shooting off about now?"

"My horse was sponged today," Jimmy said slowly. "I—"

"I was saying that a person who'd do that ought to be whipped," Dean said. His dark gaze was hard on Armsted's. "I was saying I'd like to do it."

Armsted bellowed with laughter. "Limitless can't get over a little trick he thinks I pulled at Hialeah a few seasons back."

"Let's not quarrel," Clancy Bingham said. "I want you to look over these figures, Jimmy, and see they're all correct. The way I figure it, I owe you forty-eight dollars on the horse. It's too bad he didn't win today. I don't know what I'll do with—"

DEAN and Armsted had been looking at one another. Dean said softly, cutting in on Bingham's voice, paying him no attention, "Did you have Jimmy's horse sponged today?"

Armsted chuckled so that his fat body shook. He put a cigar in his mouth without clipping the end. "What's it to you?"

"I want to know."

"Now, fellows," Clancy Bingham said querously. "Let's not—"

"Why don't you find out?" Armsted said.

There was no change in Dean's face, though he could feel the muscles growing tight. "Maybe I could," he said.

Armsted's eyes were slitted. His white hand came up and took the cigar out of his mouth, did something with it fast, and put it back in his mouth. "You mean you think you can find who stoppered this horse today—find the guy back of most of this stuff?"

"Now boys—" Bingham said.

"Perhaps," Dean said.

"Within a week, I reckon? A great man like you."

Dean didn't answer. His gaze was flat on Armsted.

The fat man reached into his pocket and took out a checkbook. He bent and wrote *Cash. Ten Thousand Dollars.* He tore the check from the book and flipped it under Dean's nose. "Put up or shut up," he said.

Persons were turning from the bar to gather around the booth now. Armsted leaned back in his seat and chuckled. "Watch *The* Limitless back water," he said. "Always shooting off his mouth until it comes to cash. Well," he flicked the check at Dean again, "how about it, Blowhard?"

It was a bad bet and Dean knew it. The odds were immeasurably against him turning up anything within a week, or ever. Armsted had purposely tried to anger him, to make him lose his head and step into a foolish gamble. But Dean had never yet let emotions dictate his bets—and then, before he could speak, Jimmy Aldrich was shaken by a spasm of coughing. He doubled over, holding the handkerchief tight against his mouth.

Dean stood up and took a wallet from his inside coat pocket. "What odds?" he said.

"Odds?" Armsted chuckled. "If you're so hot you—"

"Five to one?"

"You don't need odds. The Great Dean, you—"

"Five to one?"

"Okay. One week from tonight."

Dean counted out five hundred dollars. "The rest is at my hotel. I'll give you a note for it. The bartender can hold the stakes." He turned to Jimmy. "The bet's half yours," he said, "because you've got to help me win it. Okay?"

THE coughing spell had stopped, but Jimmy still held the handkerchief against his mouth, his head averted. Fnally he looked at Dean. "Thanks. You know I couldn't be of any real help. And I can't cover a share of the bet." His flushed face got suddenly stiff. "But if I could—"

"You'll do your share."

"No. I'd borrow from you Limitless; but I won't have a chance to repay you for a couple of years, maybe for—" He bit the word off. "If I had money to bet. . . ."

"Wait a minute!" Dean said "The horse is still yours, isn't he?"

"Until tonight. Mr. Bingham lent me money on him and closes tonight."

"How much?"

"Eight hundred."

"All right," Dean said. "I'll lend you the money to pay him off. I'll lend you twelve hundred on Lookout; he's worth that, isn't he?"

"Yes," Jimmy said. "But maybe you couldn't get—"

"All right," Dean said. He didn't have money that wasn't already bet, but he could get it. "Mark those bills paid and I'll give you a note for eight hundred," he told Bingham.

The little man squirmed uncomfortably. "But I—I. . . ."

"You thought you had a good horse for eight hundred bucks," Dean said.

"No. I was just doing Jimmy a favor. I swear I was. I don't know what I'd do with the horse. I—"

"Mark 'em paid," Dean said.

"I'll—I'll have to have cash."

Dean swung around, his eyes searching the crowd. He knew some of them, some he didn't. But he didn't see any big money until a man said, "Hello, Limitless. Maybe I can help."

He was a slim, middle aged man, darkly handsome and romantic looking. Dean remembered having been in a poker game with him at Saratoga one or two years before, but he couldn't remember his name. The man had his wallet in his hand. "How much do you need?" he asked.

"E i g h t hundred," Dean said. "Thanks. I'll get that for you tomorrow. I make the note to. . . ?"

"Searcy. Harry Searcy," the man said.

Dean remembered then. A plunger, a long shot gambler who, contrary to all the rules, never seemed to be broke.

Dean made out a note for four hundred to Jimmy Aldrich, and Jimmy pushed it across to Armsted. "The same five to one," he said.

Armsted hesitated. "Broke?" Dean said. "Or yellow?"

"I can cover all the money you raise," the fat man said.

Dean knew the checks were good. Armsted wasn't the man to get in trouble that way. When the bartender had put the money in his safe, Dean turned back to Jimmy. "Come on," he said. "I want to see the swipe who was supposed to be watching your horse this morning."

Armsted stood up and waved a fat arm. "Come on, boys," he yelled. "Let's all go watch him. Sherlock Dean."

For an instant Dean checked himself. But it was too late to turn back now. He and Jimmy went out with a crowd following.

AS they left two men who had been listening from the bar, men dressed like swipes, but who had been drinking Scotch whiskey, got up and followed. They didn't appear to hurry, but one of them left a half filled glass. They tagged along at the fringe of the crowd.

Jimmy was talking to Dean about his swipe. "Bill's a good fellow," he said. "Liquor's got him since he got too big to ride, but he never gets drunk before a race. He swears he wasn't away from the barn more than ten minutes all morning. And I believe him."

"Would he have done the job—if he were paid enough?"

"Hell no. He worked for Dad for ten years, rode for him when he was a punk. He wouldn't sell out."

"You kept the horse under cover," Dean said, "but somebody was afraid of him. You talked to anybody about him?"

"No. Bill's ridden him in the mornings, and he hasn't talked either. I know. But anybody may have watched him work."

The track entrance was closed to automobiles at this time of night, so the whole crowd walked. To the right lay the dark, mile oval of the track. On the left the double line of barns, an occasional light showing in a tackroom. Sometimes they could hear the nervous pacing of a horse in his stall. A group of Negroes were singing off in the darkness. A fire glowed between two of the barns. Red beans and rice, the backside special at the Fair Grounds.

"Back here," Jimmy said. "Barn thirty-five."

They went between two barns, dodging the remains of a fire where water had been heated after the races that afternoon. A goat was picketed here— every barn had its mascot. Dogs, goats, monkeys, crows. In the day time the place looked like a zoo. There was a second row of barns behind the first. "This one," Jimmy said.

The tackroom door was closed but a light showed around the edges. "Bill's probably drunk," Jimmy said.

Behind them Armsted boomed, "Now we'll watch the Great Dean detect." Somebody tittered. Jimmy pulled open the tackroom door.

Dean and Jimmy were shoulder to shoulder at the door. For a long moment neither of them moved, neither spoke. Dean's face was unchanged, dark and cynical. Jimmy's eyes were growing wild. His mouth worked dryly as he stared down at the body of his swipe.

Bill lay on the cot with bridles and saddles hanging from the wall over him. His arms were wide spread. His face looked up blankly. There was something terrible about his very stillness, and even before Dean reached him and lifted him so that he could see the knife wound under the left shoulder blade, he knew that he would never learn anything from Bill.

Bill had been murdered.

SOMETHING changed about Dean's face then, quick, and dark, and was gone again. His hand moved fast, so fast that only Jimmy and one or two of those beyond the door saw it brush over the bed under the dead man's shoulder. Then Dean put whatever he had found into his pocket and turned, saying, "Tell somebody outside to call the cops. And then shut the door."

Jimmy did. He stood backed against the wall on the far side of the room. He had seen men die often. In the Sanatarium ward where he had lain for two years the turnover had been fairly rapid. But that was death expected and waited and prepared for. This was something else. "He was—murdered?" Jimmy asked.

"Yes."

"Because of the race this afternoon?"

"I think so. But not here. There's not enough blood. He was killed somewhere else and brought here." He was

silent a moment before he turned, opened the door, and went outside.

"Well," Armsted boomed. "You got a job now, Sherlock!"

"Right," Dean said. He stood looking at the fat man, the light from the open door falling across his dark face, the mouth set a little crooked, the eyes fathomless. "I've always hated your type of gambler," he said emotionlessly. "This is going to give me more pleasure than anything in a long while." His gaze lay flat against Armsted's. "You want to double that bet?" he asked.

"Huh?"

"Double it," Dean said.

Armsted's gaze was crafty. "When I see the cash," he said. "No more notes."

From the darkness at Dean's side a man said, "I can let you have that tomorrow, Limitless—if you cut me in on a third of the bet." It was Harry Searcy.

"Thanks," Dean said. He never looked toward the plunger, keeping his gaze on Armsted. "Tomorrow at one, before the first race. At the Mystery Bar."

"Okay," Searcy said.

For a moment Armsted hesitated. "Called," he said finally.

It was two hours later, just short of midnight when the City Editor of the *Star* looked up and saw Limitless Dean across the desk. "Hello," he said. "I thought you were in the money."

"Maybe I am," Dean said.

"Then what you doing here? I never knew you to work when the dice had anything but deuces on them."

"Maybe it's just newspaper breeding," Dean said. "I think there's a story coming up, a good one, and I want to be on a paper when it breaks."

"Yeah? What is it?"

"That swipe who was murdered out at the Fair Grounds a couple of hours ago. You got that?"

"Yes."

"I think it's likely to develop into something. I want to work on it, and I want some sort of official position for doing it."

HE said that, his dark, emotionless face bent over the City Editor, in his green eyeshade, and the circle of light from the desk lamp. He was thinking, "It's because I want to pretend I'm a gambler. It's because I saw Jimmy Aldrich bet his life and more than that and be cheated out of it and grin. It's because I'm jealous of the kid and the guts he's got. It's because I want to pretend I'm half the man he is."

"Sure," the City Editor was saying. "Any time you've got a story, Limitless, you can work for me."

"Thanks," Dean said. "And add a box to the story you've got. Say one of the first men to discover the body, the first man to touch it, bet four thonsand dollars that within a week the police would know where the swipe was killed and who killed him. That bet won't be covered until early tomorrow afternoon. The police don't know of any clues that would make the gambler this optimsitic."

"Say! Who—?"

"Dón't worry about it," Dean said. "It's true." He turned and went out.

In some of the French Quarter bars, and in some out by the track, Limitless Dean drank Scotch and soda and kept to himself. He was carrying a small calibre gun in his inside coat pocket and he didn't like the feel of it. He didn't like the feel that he got in each new bar and in each dark street that he passed along. He found that his mouth was dry. The liquor didn't wet it, and didn't stimulate him. He kept thinking of Jimmy Aldrich, of the stain of blood on the boy's handkerchief, of the long, slow years ahead of Jimmy with their uncertainty and terror and pain, and of the boy saying, "I'm sorry. I didn't mean to tout you on a flop."

News had run wild through the track bars. Dean kept to himself, though he let them know that anybody with money could get it covered; but he didn't have the reputation of being an easy man to beat, and the gamblers kept off him.

The street leading to Dean's apartment hotel was dark with tree shadows and it was late when Dean turned down it.

A figure broke from the shadows suddenly, close at his side. "You Limitless Dean?" the man asked. He was one of the two swipes who had been in the Mystery Bar earlier that night.

"Yes," Dean said.

"You bet a lot of money," the man said. "You sure you gonna win?"

"I made the bets," Dean said.

The man pulled Dean back into thick shadows. He was afraid and it showed in his eyes and the movements of his hands. "What'll you pay for a tip?"

"That depends on the tip," Dean said.

The man looked up and down the deserted street. His teeth were chattering. "Listen," he whispered. "The cops know Bill was knocked off inside the track, but they ain't never gonna be able to search all the barns for bloodstains. If you knew which barn. . . ."

"Two hundred bucks," Dean said.

"It's worth more'n that. You got down four grand at five to one. I heard you."

"Two hundred," Dean said. "And you're not worth it. I can break the case without you."

"And you get twenty grand," the man said. "I didn't know you were cheap."

"You want it?"

"I gotta take it. Hand it over."

"When I see the bloodstains," Dean said.

THE man hesitated. He was more frightened than ever. Even in the dark his eyes had a crazy glint, and Dean thought he got the odor of marijuana. "All right," he said at last. "Come on. Back this way."

The track was only two blocks distant. They went down Leda and turned right to where there was a gate that should have been locked, but wasn't. There was no guard here. "This way," the swipe said. By now Dean was sure they were being followed.

There was fog rising over the low ground, so that the barns showed vaguely distorted. It was silent here, with no sound of horses. "Over here. This barn," the swipe whispered. "Be quiet."

Dean remembered then. Two months before barns at this end of the Fair Grounds had been partially destroyed by fire and most of them were still vacant. "Here," the swipe said. They were at the front end of a barn, between tackroom and stalls, where the building is cut straight through from side to side. It was utterly dark.

"All right," the swipe said. His voice had changed. "What'd you find under Bill's corpse?" Less than two feet away he crouched over an automatic.

"Not *what* it was," Dean said. He spoke as though he had been expecting the question, waiting for it; but the pain in his heart was almost unbearable and his lungs had ceased to work. "It's where I've put it and how you'll get it back. That's what counts. And if you shoot, you'll have the whole track on you before you can get away."

"Where is it?" the man said again. He was panting like an animal.

"I'll show you," Dean said. He reached for his inside coat pocket.

Close behind him, inside the barn, came the swift rush of sound. Dean whirled. Out of the darkness the man plunged, a knife lashing down.

Limitless Dean could deal cards so swiftly they came from the pack in a continuous flood, the movements of his wrist almost invisible. His hand moved that way now, swinging the .25 automatic in the same instant that he dived sideways. He fired once, and his gun muzzle was nearly touching the knifeman's chest. And while he was still moving the swipe who had brought him began to shoot.

Dean was skidding, sliding in damp straw, and he went down hard, rolling. He was inside the barn, the gunman showing dully against the darkness outside, his gun making sharp red stabs at the night. Dean fired again. The man outside screamed and was gone, running.

Limitless Dean got to his knees. He was breathing hard and his stomach felt weak. "Damn," he said. "I—" Close behind him, shrouded in the utter darkness, a third gun boomed.

The bullet lashed glancing across Dean's temple, slammed him face down. He lay there, conscious, but paralyzed. The gun had slipped from his fingers.

He heard steps in the darkness behind him, close by, coming forward. They were short, shuffling steps. He knew that against the wet straw, in this darkness, he was invisible. But the killer was searching for him.

DEAN'S hand groped cautiously at the straw. If he could find his own gun . . . He had no idea whether he had dropped it straight down as he fell, or instinctively raised his arm and in that way tossed it forward. His fingers pawed silently in the straw—and found nothing.

The steps were inches away. Closer . . . Something kicked his leg. And still the shocked, bullet-caused paralysis held Dean motionless.

In the darkness a man began to

cough, the cough of tuberculosis.

It seemed to Dean that time stopped, hung motionless, and there was no world except that terrible coughing.

Close at Dean's feet something moved in the straw. A gun spat.

And at the same moment the paralysis left the gambler. He twisted, still flat on his belly. His flailing hands caught a leg and he jerked. A man crashed down on top of him. It was a wild and frantic groping of arms and legs. A gun boomed. Then Dean got a grip on the gun and wrenched it and swung it twice. The man he fought with went limp.

The coughing had stopped. In the barn there was utter silence. Then Jimmy's voice called, "Limitless!"

"You damn fool," Dean said. He stood up, panting and feeling sick at his stomach. "You're supposed to be home in bed."

"I was," Jimmy said, "but I got to thinking. After you left, a swipe asked me what you found under Bill's body. He acted scared. And after I got to bed I kept thinking maybe somebody would try to kill you for what you'd found. I went over to your place and got there in time to see you and this guy coming here. I—I followed."

"Thanks," Dean said. "Now go home and to bed."

"It was Clancy Bingham," Dean told Jimmy the next day. "He had a couple of swipes doing the dirty work for him. You'd had to toot your horse up as no ordinary claiming plater to get Bingham to loan you the eight hundred He didn't know how good Lookout was, but he'd fixed that race for another horse to win, and he took no chances."

"Did you know it was him?"

"I knew you must have talked your horse up to him. But that wasn't any proof. However, the swipe that I wounded last night was caught and he nearly broke his jaw trying to lay all the blame on Bingham, and Bingham sprained his tongue blaming the swipe I killed."

"For Bill's murder?"

"Yes. This swipe, the wounded one, went by and got Bill to have a beer while the other one sponged Lookout. Bill got to thinking about that later and he got drunk and mad and started looking for the swipe. That's their story and probably true. Bill found all three of them together and raised so much hell that somebody, probably Bingham, got excited and killed him."

DEAN'S mouth was in that half bitter smile. "It was a good gamble," he said. "Armsted won't pay off the second bet, but I make ten grand out of him and you get two thousand and your horse."

"Not the horse," Jimmy said. "I owe you twelve hundred for the horse."

"Not me. Nobody may agree with me, but I think I'm worth more than that damned horse. And you saved my life last night. I'll swap you that for the horse."

Jimmy said, "Wait a minute. What was it you found under Bill's body?"

"Nothing," Dean said.

"Nothing?"

"Not a damn thing. But I knew that people outside would think I had. So I went out and doubled my bets to make it look good. I didn't know if the real killer was there, but I knew how gossip gets around the back of the racetrack. And anyway I went down and got it in the paper to make sure. What helped was that Bingham actually had lost a stick pin. He was afraid I'd found that."

"You mean you purposely —— you wanted 'em to try. . . ."

"It was just a first card bluff," Dean said. "It made 'em think I had something in the hole. And if it failed, I still had the rest of the week to draw a pair."

O HANDSOME—THE COPS!

by JAMES DUNCAN

Author of "Green Ice to Cool a Coffin," etc.

Maybe I'm getting soft in the cranium, but it strikes me as damn queer that a couple of guys would fight to the death over a jar of my Gracie's cold cream!

I says well, this is where knowing jiu-jitsu comes in handy

I HAD just englished a money ball into the side pocket when Eddie says O Handsome, you are being paged by your big moment. She has hung up her face betwen them swinging doors. I flipped a look.

It was Gracie and she was wig-wagging distress signals at me.

Whoops! Down went my cue and on went my coat and when I was outside I says Gracie honey we ain't married yet and here you are keeping tabs on me. What will the boys think?

She took my arm and shiggered in close like only she really knows how and says O Handsome I am not keeping tabs on you but I had to see you because an awful thing has happened. Somebody stole my cold cream jar and I am scared.

I says what's to be scared about a thing like that? She says why, you do not understand, it was not the cold cream that scared me. It was the two masked men, she says.

Gracie toots, I says, you know that I love you but please, please do not always tell a story back-end frontwards, it is very confusing. What two masked men?

Why, the two masked men with the guns, she says. They came into the shop while I was in the back washing up. Only Mr. Allegrini was up front, the other two barbers had gone home. Mr. Allegrini was just going to close up when the two men came in with guns.

I says O a stick-up, eh? Did they hurt you and how much did they grab? But Gracie says it was not a stick-up. They did not hurt anyone and they did not grab anything. They were looking for the cold cream jar, she says.

What cold cream jar, I says. Why, she says, the jar that stood on the glass shelf over my table. It was there all week, I only bought it last Saturday, and it was three-quarters full and it cost me a dollar and a half. But when the two masked men looked for it, it was gone.

Gracie sweets, I says, I love you. I mean I really do. But do you mean to stand here and tell me two guys went to all the trouble of using masks and guns just to look for a jar of cold cream in a barber shop. What did they want, I says, a facial? O, Gracie says getting mad, so you think I am making this up do you, and I says well sugar it is easier to take that way, I should hate to think my best girl was squiffed.

She says you are like all the rest of them, there is no use talking sense to men. Mr. Allegrini, she says, was right there and he told the cops a different story and the cops would not believe what I told them. I says please Gracie do not cry.

She says Handsome, if you do not want I should cry, please come back to the shop with me and tell them cops where they get off not believing what I

told them. It is not justice to tell a girl she did not see or hear what she saw and heard with her own eyes and ears.

So just to humor her we walked to the hotel which was only a few blocks from the billiard parlor and went through the lobby to where the barber shop was and at the door was a cop. I says cop, what has been going on around here? He says who wants to know? I says I do. He says all right, make a noise like a hoop and roll away. I says cop, it is a good thing you wear a uniform and that I have respect for the law. Otherwise I would show you a trick or two in jiu-jitsu. Yeah, he says, you and who else? Get away from here or you will get it where the bottle got the cork.

Gracie says O Handsome show him what you showed that fresh lifeguard at Coney Island last summer, and I might have showed him something like that all right because that is a very good trick, but just then a guy in plainclothes with dick written all over his thick mugg came out of the door and says what is the trouble around here?

BUT then he saw Gracie and he says O, O, no trouble, just that dame again. Lady, he says, you chewed our ears off once, so now go home like a good girl and leave us alone. You are the dizziest blonde I ever did see. I says now dick, you got no call to speak to Gracie like this. She is only trying to help you. O yeah who are you, says the dick.

I says my name is Albert Tripp, but my friends call me Handsome. I am head bell-hop in this hotel and this is my night off. Yes, says Gracie, and he came back with me to make you listen to the truth of what happened with the two masked men and the cold cream jar. I says Gracie honey pipe down and let me handle this will you, and the dick says Brother I know just how you feel. But if you can shut her up, you're a better man than I am. Are you married to this dame?

Not yet, I says, but we will be when we have enough saved up which will be in about six months. I says we want to get our furniture for cash. That way we know it is ours. No time payment installment plans for us, I says. Cash for all we buy, I says. That is the goal Gracie and I have set ourselves, and the dick says to the cop six more months to live. The cop says O, O it is a pity, he is so young too. What do you mean young, I says, I am twenty-six. What are you guys talking about? And Gracie says do not mind them Handsome, these dumb cops are just trying to kid people. Ask him about the two masked men and I says to the dick well, what about them?

Mr. Allegrini came to the door and when he saw Gracie he made a face like he had a stomach-ache. Mr. Allegrini wears very good clothes and always smells of perfume like a woman. He is an elegant man and very slick. I mean he looks like money, even though he is only a head barber. He says Gracie you are the best manicurist my shop ever had but what do you use for brains? Please go home and do not trouble what's under your permanent any more about what happened in the shop tonight. Let bygones be bygones. I says just a minute, were there or were there not two masked men with guns in here?

The dick says sure there were two masked men with guns. She saw them all right because they really were here. But she insists they were looking for a jar of cold cream. I says you mean they weren't, and the dick says well, what do you think, why should two stick-up men want cold cream. That is what I thought, I says, and I gave Gracie a funny look. Mr. Allegrini says after all gentlemen I was here all the

time and I did not hear anything about cold cream. This is becoming a farce.

O Handsome says Gracie I am insulted. She says Mr. Allegrini I am a lady and I hate to call you a liar. But she says you are a liar. You know as well as I do that the two masked men were looking for a cold cream jar. Mr. Allegrini did things to his hair. It looked like he was tearing at it. Gracie he says you are fired. Do not come into my shop again. You are a disgrace to me and to my shop's good name. I never want to see you again.

Before Gracie could say a word I says now Mr. Allegrini please. Please do not fire Gracie, I says. I will hear no more of it, says Mr. Allegrini. Get away from here before I scream, he says. The two of you are enough to drive a man cuckoo. I says please reconsider Mr. Allegrini. Mr. Allegrini got purplish and his eyes popped and he tried to get a lot of words out all at once so they got stuck in his throat inside and he gurgled. Finally he says in a small weak voice Officer get these people away from here or arrest them. They are disturbing my peace, he says. The cop poked me with his thumb in the chest and says git Buddy git. I says very well I do not choose to make a public scene. We will depart without your help cop and take your dirty thumb out of my chest, I says.

So I took Gracie's arm and led her away and we sat down in a corner of the lobby. She was like in a daze. She says O Handsome this is awful, maybe I have been wrong all along. After all, she says, it is not reasonable for a man like Mr. Allegrini to lie for nothing about a thing like a jar of cold cream. I says Gracie baby now you are talking sense. But after a minute she says yes but who stole my cold cream. I says I give up toots. Now you got me doing it. Maybe it was vanishing cream.

Just then a little man with blonde

hair and a pair of enormous specs on his eyes comes over and he says how do you do. I am Mr. Anderson, here is my card. I took it and said I am Albert Tripp but people call me Handsome for short and this is Gracie my fiancee. We are glad to meet you. I read the card. It said

> PAUL ANDERSON
> representing
> Better Times Insurance Company, Inc.

Mr. Anderson says I am glad to know you.

Well, I says Mr. Anderson I am not in the field for insurance at this time. I says of course a man should provide for the future but Gracie has a cousin who sells insurance and I promised him my business when I get ready to buy. Mr. Anderson bobbed his head and the specs which were too big for him wobbled up and down his nose, and says I understand perfectly but tell me what happened in the barber shop.

SO Gracie told him everything that happened and he was very sympathetic. It is too bad you have lost your job, he says, and it is too bad the police choose to believe Mr. Allegrini and not you. I am very sorry the police are so shortsighted, he says, and thank you very very much. You are welcome, I says. Goodbye, says Mr. Anderson and thank you very very much. He says it was a pleasure to meet you and I says likewise. He started to walk away and I says say goodbye to Mr. Anderson Gracie.

But she was not listening because she was deep in thought. After a few minutes she says O Handsome do you remember Pinky Martin? Do I, I says, now listen Gracie lamb let us not start off on that again. He is a bum and I will not even talk about him.

This Pinky Martin is a guy who lived in the hotel and what a chief bell-hop does not know about the people living in a hotel is not worth knowing. Well, this Pinky Martin got sweet on Gracie and once he took her out to a show and a whirl. They got intimate because Pinky used the shop for manicures and shaves. Gracie and I had quite a fight about it but it was all patched up. I had convinced her he was just a bum.

So I says well, anyway Pinky Martin doesn't live here any more. He checked out for Miami last week. And Gracie says he is here again because I saw him in the shop tonight about an hour before the stickup. He has taken the same room in the hotel. I says now Gracie but she cut in and says I only thought of him because he mentioned the cold cream while I was giving him a manicure. He asked me if I used a lot of cold cream to keep my hands so soft and I says O only a little now and then. I says well, what has that got to do with it. But she got up and says we will go talk to Pinky. What for, I says. To check up on that jar of cold cream, she says. Why, she says Pinky must have seen the jar standing on the shelf. He can tell me if I'm crazy or not.

He ain't no Solomon, I says. But Gracie did not hear me because she was already in the elevator and I had to chase to get in with her. Frank, the elevator cowboy, says you must love this place Handsome to come here on your night off. What floor? I says look Frank, this is all Gracie's idea. Make it the sixth. He says I did not know Gracie had an idea.

So we got out at the sixth and walked to six-o-nine. That was the room Pinky Martin had had before. I knocked on the door and Gracie primped her hair to fluff it out above the ears. No one answered the knock, so Gracie took hold of the knob to rattle it. The knob turned and the door opened and Gracie says we might just as well look in.

She went in first and came down on her heels hard as though she were going to faint. I caught her as she started going back and looked over her shoulder.

A guy was laying on the floor, one cheek hugging the rug and with his legs drawn up to his stomach like he was asleep. Only he wasn't asleep. You could tell that by the blood on his head and on the rug. His hair was wet and greasy-looking with blood. O, I says, it's Pinky Martin. He has come to a bad end.

Gracie made funny sounds in her throat and was terribly white, so I pushed her down into a chair. But she says O Handsome look over there on the writing table. I looked. A lot of newspaper had been spread over the table and on the newspaper was plastered a heap of cold cream from a jar that stood next to it. Everything in that jar had been scooped out onto the newspaper, and it was a lot of cold cream. O, Gracie says, there you are, that is my jar of cold cream. I did not know Pinky Martin was a cheap sneak-thief.

I says Gracie are you sure it is your jar. Of course I am sure, she says. It is Moon Blossom brand, ain't it? Well, that's my brand and that's my jar. Why, she says Pinky must have stolen it off the shelf when I went back to get a pan of hot water to soak his fingers and soften his cuticle.

This is certainly peculiar, I says. What on earth would he want with a jar of cold cream? Well, Gracie says, I am certainly disappointed in Mr. Pinky Martin. I thought he was a gentleman. The idea of stealing a jar of cold cream from a girl that cost a dollar and a half. I certainly would like to give Mr. Pinky Martin a piece of my mind.

I says Gracie lambkins I am afraid you are too late for that because I am afraid Mr. Pinky Martin is no longer with the living. She let out a yeep and says you mean he is dead. Well, I says, if he ain't, he is giving a damned good

imitation of it. Anyway, I says, you can get your job back from Mr. Allegrini now because he will be sorry he fired you when he hears how wrong he was about the jar of cold cream. Well, that is something, says Gracie, there is never a cloud without a silver lining. But, she says, I am certainly disappointed in Mr. Pinky Martin.

A VOICE says so are we chicken. I flipped my head around and there was the closet door opening and two men coming out. One of them says you stand by the door Egg-Head in case these tootsies think they want out. Okay Carl says the other and he laughed and moved to the door and the fellow named Carl laughed and Gracie says if you'd tell me the joke I would laugh too. What is so funny here anyway? Ixnay Gracie I says. Ixnay now. Please let me do the talking.

Then I says Boys let us sit down and talk this over. This is no need to use violence. Carl laughed harder and he says that is exactly what Pinky told us and now look at him. Well, says Gracie, that is not so very funny, if you ask me. Who asked you, says Egg-Head. Shut up and speak when you're spoken to. I think, he says to Carl, these young people are tired of living. I hate to look at their faces because they look so tired. Gracie says mister, your face is nothing to brag about so I would not talk so fresh. In fact, she says, I think your face is like a custard pie without the custard.

I says Gracie lamb please button your lip and let me handle this situation. Well, I do not see why I have to take any lip off of strange men, Gracie says. What is the matter with you, Handsome, she says. You act like you were scared of these half-pints. Well, I says, strictly on the q. t. Gracie these boys have their hands in their right-hand pockets and unless I am very much mistaken there are guns in those pockets. If I act as though I were scared, I says, that is why. Furthermore, I says, these boys are not wearing any masks, but if they were I think you would recognize them.

Gracie's mouth opened a little and her face screwed up and she says O Handsome these are the two stick-up men. Well, I says, you catch on mighty quick. The fellow named Carl moved over nearer to us and he says now let us get to the bottom of this. Is that your jar of cold cream on the writing table?

Why, of course, says Gracie. I told the cops you were after the jar but Mr. Allegrini insisted I was imagining the whole thing or something and then he fired me because he said I was trying to make him out a lunatic. Well, this only proves I was right and Mr. Allegrini wrong and it goes to show that a man who cannot remember what his own ears heard is a man who . . .

Egg-Head butted in and says Sister hold it. You have proven your case. He turned and says that is so, ain't it, Carl, and Carl says well it looks that way to me. I says look Boys, Gracie and me don't understand a thing about this and I don't know as we want to. O, says Gracie, is that so? I should certainly like to find out what it is all about, if you don't mind. Would you, says Egg-Head. I certainly would, says Gracie. Okay, says Egg-Head, pick yourself a spot because I am going to drop you.

About now the door to the hall swings open behind Egg-Head and the little guy with the specs named Mr. Anderson sticks his face in and yells. Suddenly there is a lot of noise and running and shooting. I could not see much of it because I was down on the floor and I had pulled Gracie down and I was sitting on her, so she would not get into no trouble or stop any of the wild bullets zinging around. It kept up real wild for about five minutes or maybe longer and then suddenly it is all quiet again.

I sent a peeper up over the arm of a chair and there is the little guy sitting on the floor all by his lonesome and Egg-Head and Carl are gone. The little guy is looking at his gun awful solemn, squinting at it kind of, and I says what is the difficulty Mr. Anderson, and he says I lost my specs and could not see worth a darn and them dirty so-and-so's have taken a powder. With my specs on I could have blasted them to smithereens. Are you hurt, I says. No, he sez, but help me find my specs. I am blind without them. He was pawing around on the floor and cursing and I says please Mr. Anderson there is a lady present and he says excuse me. I found his specs and he put them on and by that time there were a lot of people in the room, including a cop. In fact, it was the same cop as had been standing at the door of the barber shop.

Gracie and I went over and shook hands with Mr. Anderson and she says you saved our lives and if you want to you can be best man at our wedding. Can't he, Handsome? I says you bet. Mr. Anderson looked like he was awful pleased and then he got red to the ears because Gracie gave him a smackerino of a kiss right in front of everybody.

WELL, says the cop, what has been the trouble here? I says there was no trouble, just two fresh stick-up guys who tried to murder me and Gracie. They murdered Pinky Martin and if you look over there you can see the cold cream jar that was stolen from Gracie. Right now, I says, we are on our way to tell Mr. Allegrini he has got to give Gracie back her job. Mr. Allegrini has gone home, says the cop. Your story does not hang together.

O, I says, it doesn't, eh? I says cop, you took care to come here after the shooting was over. You did not come rushing in when the guns were popping, now did you. So do not high-hat me with any third-degree.

Yes, Gracie says, you would not believe me when I said my cold cream was stolen. Now you can see it with your own eyes. Listen, says the cop, to hell with cold cream. There is a dead man lying here and it looks like murder and do not mention cold cream to me again or I will commit murder, so help me.

Mr. Anderson got hold of the cop's arm and led him away and said something in a whisper. The cop looked over at Gracie in a very peculiar way and then he nodded his head and says okey. He was nicer after that and smiling at Gracie. Then he got out a little book and we had to tell him everything that happened and he wrote it down just as we told it to him. Then he says you kids can run along and play now. Go home, get out, one two, skidoo. I says never mind the bum's rush cop, we can take a hint, and Gracie says this place is getting on my nerves Handsome. If there is anything I hate it is dumb cops. That stuck him and he had no answer.

We went out then and were walking down the corridor and suddenly I stopped and saw that Gracie had run back to six-o-nine and was hanging her face in the door. I went back and says what is the idea of running back Gracie and she says I am making woogle-eyes and woggle-mouth at that dumb cop just to get even. He is trying to look dignified but he cannot take it and in about a minute he will froth at the mouth. Mr. Anderson is holding him back. I think Mr. Anderson is a very nice man, she says, don't you?

Well, when we got down to the street I says let's catch the subway home. Brooklyn will seem like a quiet Paradise after all the excitement around here. But Gracie says ain't you forgot something? I says what and she says

Handsome, we got to see Mr. Allegrini and have him give me my job back.

I says tomorrow morning will do. It is too late now. Well, says Gracie, if that is all our future means to you, okey by me. I says what do you mean to insinuate and she says I am not insinuating a thing only you know as well as I do that we will never save up enough in our joint bank account to buy furniture for cash unless I can pitch in a few dollars each week and if I don't have a job, how can I pitch in.

I says where does Mr. Allegrini live? Gracie says it is an apartment house on Seventy-first near Broadway. I do not remember the number but the apartment is on the third floor. Well, I says, how can we go if you do not know the number. I remember the house, she says, on account it had two lions in front of it. I went there once when Mr. Allegrini had the sneezes and could not come to the shop. What sneezes, I says and she says it is a fever from hay.

So we took the subway uptown and got out at Seventy-second Street and sure enough there was the house with two lions in front of it. A colored man took us up in the elevator. Gracie went straight to the apartment door and rang the bell. After a few minutes the door opened and Mr. Allegrini stuck his face out. My God, he says, you again, and he began to talk very fast in Italian like he was getting a lot of things off his chest. I did not like the sound of what he said even though I did not understand a word of it. I says that will do Mr. Allegrini. If you got to make a dirty crack, make it in English, I says. We only came to tell you that you were all wrong about the jar of cold cream.

What jar, he says, what are you talking about. I sez Pinky Martin stole the jar while Gracie was not looking. Then two guys killed him. They are the same two guys who stuck up the shop. We found the jar in the room where Pinky was killed, I says. So now you have got to give Gracie back her job because she was right and you were wrong and she is sorry she called you a liar.

Yes, Gracie says, I am sorry. But really Mr. Allegrini, she says, you should do something about your ears because you do not hear so good. Otherwise you would have heard those two men speaking about the jar of cold cream. Now, please, I says. Please Gracie. Mr. Allegrini does not care to have his ears discussed in public. Well what about it Mr. Allegrini, I says. Gracie is worried about getting back her job.

SO Pinky Martin was killed, says Mr. Allegrini. Do the cops know who did it? Gracie says I will never be late again Mr. Allegrini and I will do everything you tell me. Please say I am not fired. Mr. Allegrini says you are nuts.

Just then we heard the elevator stop at the floor and then the door closing. Footsteps came around a bend in the corridor and then there was Egg-Head and behind him was Carl. Mr. Allegrini squeaked like a mouse. Egg-Head and Carl began running toward us. I gave Gracie a push and she went into Mr. Allegrini and both of them went through the door. I was right behind them all the time. I tried to slam the door shut but Carl got his foot in the way and Egg-Head slammed into the door with his shoulder while I was still leaning against it.

After I got up off the floor Carl and Egg-Head were inside and they had closed and locked the door and they had their guns in their fists. Well, well, says Egg-Head, isn't this jolly? We are always running into each other. Quite a coincidence.

Carl had hurt his foot keeping the door from closing and he was hopping on the other and looking like he hurt all over. He says these kids need taking apart. Then we can see what makes them tick. Well, says Egg-Head, it would only be humane to put them out of their suffering. We will come to them later, says Egg-Head. Well, Mr. Allegrini, he says, are you surprised to see us.

Mr. Allegrini looked terribly frightened. He says what do you want. Get out of my house or I will call the cops. I do not know what you want of me, he says. O yes you do, says Egg-Head. Do you hand it over quietly or do we have to learn you. We mean business. Hit him on the schnozzle, says Carl. That will learn him. He is a sweet-smelling Wop and soft like a woman, says Carl.

O, says Mr. Allegrini, please do not hurt me. I have done nothing. You got me wrong. I have never harmed no one. O, says Egg-Head, a wise guy, eh? Don't try to play Carl and me for suckers. But I do not know what you want, says Mr. Allegrini.

Gracie says I think it is a shame to treat a good man like Mr. Allegrini the way you are treating him. I cannot stand by quietly and see you frightening him. It is not justice to act so tough to the poor man. I says Gracie honey, please. Please do not interfere. This is a business for a man. Please shut up, I says.

Egg-Head says it can't be true. I'm dreaming. Pinch me, Carl, he says. I have never met anything like this pair before for laughs. Carl says to hell with horse-ing around. I am fed up listening to these kids. He says, Mr. Allegrini, this is your last chance. Cough up or take it in the guts. He held the gun pointed at Mr. Allegrini.

Mr. Allegrini dropped to his knees and begins praying. Sweat is pouring from his face. O Handsome, says Gracie, this is a shame. She put herself in front of Mr. Allegrini, and says don't you dare touch him. Carl got red in the face. He pushed at Gracie's face and left a red mark on her cheek with his fingers showing. Get out of the way he says or your blonde noodle will get a slug smack in the middle of it. I am reaching the end of my patience, he says. O Handsome, Gracie says.

I says that was not a nice thing to do, mister. A man should never hit a lady. He says, O no? I says No. You tried rough stuff once before and it did not work. It will not work this time either, I says. He says again, O no? I says no. I says I am not one to lose my temper but you have gone too far. Well, Buddy, he says, this is where you get off. Last stop. He raised up his gun and pointed it at me. I says well, this is where knowing jiu-jitsu comes in handy. You should have known better than to get rough with Gracie. I can stand for a lot, I says, but not for that.

I chopped my wrist at his forearm just like I had been taught and danced off to the side of him. His gun went off with the reflex action but the bullet slammed into the floor. Then I got one hand over his shoulder and grabbed him by the thigh with the other and heaved. He upset like an apple-cart and did a half-flip in the air. It was just like I had done that time to the life-guard at Coney Island who had gotten fresh with Gracie. Only the life-guard had come down on sand. Carl came down on a hard floor on his shoulder and head.

EGG-HEAD began screaming and dancing around and then he cut loose with his coffee roaster and hot flame spurted from it. Mr. Allegrini seemed very much surprised. He says, Ah! and began to slide toward the floor.

I says get your head down, Gracie. Then I feinted at Egg-Head's left. Two slugs went screaming by my ear. I could have put my initials on them, they were that close. But they missed which was all I cared about. Gracie was screaming O, be careful, Handsome. I got hold of the wrist of Egg-Head's gun hand and then clamped down on his forearm just below the elbow joint. He says leggo, you are breaking my arm. And he strains away from me. I says the idea is exactly that, only it is your wrist, not your arm, according to my instructions.

Something snapped and made a funny sort of sound and Egg-Head screamed and went limp against me. I let him fall to the floor. He had fainted. Then I gathered up his gun and Carl's and stuck them into my pocket.

Someone was trying to kick in the door, so I says, Gracie honey, please see who it is. O Handsome, she says, are you hurt? Not a scratch. It was nothing. Them guys pushed me too far. It was their fault for starting it, I says.

Then she went to the door and opened it and it was the guy with the specs, Mr. Anderson. I was sure surprised to see him and he was even more surprised to see us.

What hit, he says, a tornado. What are you kids doing here? We just came to ask Mr. Allegrini to give Gracie her job back, I says. Then these two monkeys got tough. Yes, says Gracie, and Handsome showed them where to get off. She told Mr. Anderson everything that happened.

His eyes opened wide. He says, what is the matter? You look pale. I tried to smile and I says it is just that I am scared. He had another look at Carl and Egg-Head and he says you are what. I says scared. I get that way when things are over, worrying over what might have happened. It was always like that even when I was a kid, I says. I tried to get over it but I never could. I guess it will follow me through life. It's my fate, I says.

Whoops, says Mr. Anderson, look at Mr. Allegrini. He is bleeding like a stuck pig. Mr. Allegrini sure looked in a bad way. His face was a pasty-gray and his lips were blue. There was a dark wet spot on his chest. He began coughing and blood bubbled from between his bluish lips. Get on a phone, Mr. Anderson says, and call an ambulance. Also the cops. Right away. He knelt beside Mr. Allegrini and got out a note-book and a pencil and I ran to the phone with Gracie beside me.

The doorway was filled with people when I turned from the phone but Mr. Anderson shooed them away and closed the door. He says it is all over with poor Mr. Allegrini. He has paid the price. I looked over and Mr. Allegrini was not moving any more. Mr. Anderson says he has confessed everything. Come, have a look.

We followed him into a bedroom and Mr. Anderson began using a pen knife on the box spring. After a little while he takes something out and cups it in the palm of his hand and says, look.

It was a green stone, kind of like a big pebble, only you could sort of look deep into it like it was a well and there were lights flashing from it. Well, says Gracie, what is it? It looks like a diamond but a diamond ain't green. It is an emerald, says Mr. Anderson in a whisper like he was in church. Ain't it a beauty?

It is all right I says. I am saving up to buy Gracie a knocker, I says, only it will not be green but blue-white like they advertise for $64.98. Mr. Anderson laughs and says maybe you could afford to buy Gracie a more expensive stone. I says how and he says well, maybe I had better tell the whole thing from the beginning.

Pinky Martin, he says, and Egg-Head and Carl are notorious jewel thieves. They snagged this emerald from Mrs. Harrison Forbes' collection.

My company carries the insurance on the stone. It is my business to keep people like Pinky Martin under watch. So I was waiting in the lobby of his hotel when he slipped in. He recognized me and knew I was going to frisk him. So he hot-footed it into the barber shop and made out he wanted a manicure. That was last week on Saturday evening.

Yes, says Gracie, I remember it perfectly. It was on Friday. I says Gracie sugar you just heard Mr. Anderson say it was Saturday. Now please do not interrupt and let him tell his story and she says well, if I pride myself on anything, it is my memory. It was on Friday.

WELL, anyway, says Mr. Anderson I did not follow Pinky into the shop. I waited for him to come out. And right there was where I made my mistake. You see, says Mr. Anderson, Pinky took the opportunity when he was certain no one was looking and cached the emerald deep down at the bottom of the cold cream jar that stood on a little glass shelf above the manicuring table.

Gracie says how do you know he did that? Mr. Allegrini just told me, says Mr. Anderson. Well, how did he know, says Gracie. I'm coming to that, says Mr. Anderson. Well, when Pinky came out all manicured I gave him the frisk and he hee-hawed at me. He told he was clean and going to Miami for a vacation. I couldn't hold him and I couldn't call in the cops, Mr. Anderson says. Pinky had help on the emerald job and I thought it was best to let him go and let him think I was completely fooled because that way I might get a line on his confederates. Well, he went away but not to Miami. We had him trailed as far as Richmond where he stopped for a couple of days and then he came back.

I had been waiting around the hotel all the time, Mr. Anderson says, hoping for a break. Pinky took his old room back and I thought he had hidden the emerald somewhere there. Then Carl and Egg-Head paid him a call. They had been his buddies on the Forbes' emerald job and they had come for their whack. Well, you can figure out the rest.

I looked at Gracie and she looked at me. I says I do not know what you mean. Please tell us what happened next.

Well, says Mr. Anderson, Pinky stole that cold cream jar off Gracie's shelf, thinking it still contained the emerald. He went upstairs to show it to his pals and when they went through it, it was just cold cream but no emerald. Get it? His pals thought maybe the jar had been switched. That's why they stuck up Gracie and Mr. Allegrini. They thought maybe there was another jar or two of the same stuff around the shop. There wasn't. So they went to work on Pinky, thinking by that time that he was holding out on them. They hit him over the head and hit him a bit too hard. He couldn't tell them what had happened to the emerald because he did not know and they got sore.

I says but what happened to the emerald? And then suddenly I says gosh I know. Mr. Allegrini fished it out.

Mr. Anderson says Handsome, that is perfectly correct. I got it all written down here as Mr. Allegrini's dying confession. He was shaving a customer, the other two barbers were busy too and Gracie was getting her manicuring stuff together at the other end of the shop. Pinky was certain no one saw him when he sunk the emerald deep down into the cold cream. But Mr. Allegrini saw him out of the corner of a slant-wise mirror that reflected into the mirror in front of Mr. Allegrini's chair.

Everything would have ended with the emerald in Mr. Allegrini's possession but you kids were there at every turn pointing the way for Carl and Egg-Head as well as for me, Mr. Anderson says. But I says it is only right to tell you that all we wanted was to get Gracie's job back.

Yes, says Gracie, I wanted the job because we are saving up to buy furniture for cash. Mr. Anderson says Handsome and Gracie think no more of deferring your wedding day until you have saved up enough cash. You can get married tomorrow. You have done my insurance company a good deed and we will reward you. I will take care to see that all the reward money is sent to you. I says what reward money are you talking about and Mr. Anderson says my company pays a standard reward of $2,500 on information for the recovery of stolen goods insured for more than $50,000. You and Gracie are entitled to the full benefit of the $2,500.

Well, we got the money all right and Mr. Anderson was best man at our wedding and helped us pick out the furniture and a swell knocker for Gracie.

I never gave that whole night another thought and my wife—I mean Gracie of course—never spoke of it either although the newspapers got awful excited about it. Then about a month after it all happened Gracie is sitting at a picture show with me and gives me a jab and says, O, Handsome, I have been thinking and thinking. I says, Gracie, this is a moving picture. I paid to see it and hear it, not to listen to you think.

But she says you must listen, Handsome. She says you know about that funny business with Pinky Martin and Mr. Allegrini and the cold cream and the emerald. I just got it figured out. Yeah, I says, what? I have just got it figured out she says that it was Saturday, not Friday. Mr. Anderson was perfectly correct.

POISON IS FOR RATS
by ORLANDO RIGONI

Author of "Line Riders of Forgotten Range," etc.

Only one guy had to be bumped off—but there was poison enough for three!

Into the first glass he poured b o t h Scotch and poison

"STICKPIN" BRADY stirred up the fire on the grate and rose to his well-groomed height. The snapping flames made glittery discs of his heavy lashed eyes. His mouth was a cruel thin line in his smooth, bluish face. From the shimmery silk of his conservative tie, the huge diamond stickpin glowed like the eye of a great cat.

There was an air of confident pride about Stickpin's tall, rather gaunt body. There was foundation for the pride. He had done rather well for himself on the borderline of crime. For the jobs he pulled, the law couldn't touch him.

The bristly, square-built man with the shaggy blond hair, who sat hulked down in one of the deep chairs of the luxurious apartment, grunted again:

"Give me a drink, Brady, I need it."

An impatient sneer flicked across

Stickpin's bluish face. "I've told you that I want you sober for tonight. I'll give you one drink when Kettleman gets here. Have you got the plane ready?"

The blond nodded. "My ship's always ready—the jobs I take don't wait." The blond frowned and added, "Where do we fly to?"

"That's none of your business, Gates. I'm paying you to take orders. I'll tell you where to go when we take off."

"Okay—okay. I've got chutes for two in the crate. . . ."

"To hell with the chutes," Stickpin snapped. An inner quiver betrayed the cowardice of the man. Even the thought of jumping from a plane unnerved him. In fact he had no love for flying, but when the stake was forty grand—well a guy had to take some chances.

He went over every detail of his plan. The liquor was on the side table. In his pocket, his prong-like fingers fumbled with the little bottle of poison. He knew just where the little black bag was with the worthless glass in it.

It was all quite simple. Kettleman was loaded up with stolen "ice." Brady had asked him to bring it up to this apartment for his inspection, with the offer to buy it if it proved satisfactory. He knew just what kind of bag Kettleman used to carry his junk in, for he had done business with Kettleman before.

His pride still rankled when he thought of the last deal he had made with the wily crook. Kettleman had tricked him into buying some second rate junk at a fancy price. Well, it wouldn't be junk tonight, and it was going to be clear profit for Stickpin Brady. Kettleman was too wise to live, anyway.

Brady drew out his thin gold watch. Eight-thirty. As though his movement had been a signal, the buzzer rasped out its imperative order.

Brady scowled at the blond, bulked down in the chair. "Don't open your yap, see? I'm paying you for flying a plane, because I've never been in one before. You're just my bodyguard, see?"

The blond nodded jerkily. "Let the guy in, I'm dyin' for that drink."

Stickpin Brady went to the front door of the apartment and opened it to admit a fleshy, pock-marked man who seemed to have no neck, and whose eyes were beady circles imbedded in flesh.

"Come in, Kettleman," Brady said crisply, his eyes noting with satisfaction the black bag the pouchy man carried in his gloved hand.

"Glad to see you're ready for business, Brady," Kettleman rasped, a cheshire grin expanding his rubbery mouth. "Whose the bloke inside?"

Stickpin said carelessly, "A guard I hired, Kettleman. I'm getting nervous about these deals. Take tonight, for instance. I'd be a pushover for some smart rat."

Kettleman's fat face clouded. "You don't trust me, Brady?" he said belligerently.

Brady soothed him, "No, not that. Some outsider could jimmy his way in here and make off with the ice and the money, too."

"Nobody tails me when I don't want to be tailed," Kettleman said flatly, and followed Brady into the dimly lit sitting room.

THE blond aviator didn't move as they entered. He was thinking, too. There was good money in flying when you weren't particular what kind of jobs you picked up. Take this job, for instance. He might be able to make a nice profit on it. Brady wouldn't wear a chute. All right. Suppose they did get away with the loot. What was to stop him, Gates, from dumping Brady out when they were over the mountains and making off with the loot for himself?

Brady would have a gun handy, of course, but a few corkscrew stunts with the ship, and a man of Brady's caliber would forget about the gun—forget it long enough. . . .

Brady's voice seemed to explode in Gates' thoughts. "Come up here, Gates, and see some real dewdrops."

Gates shambled over and sat at the table with the other two. The black bag was open at Kettleman's feet, and on the table was spread out a dazzling assortment of fire.

Brady's eyes seemed to catch the sparkle of the gems and reflect it, cold, glittery. His breath sucked in with a hissing sound.

"Looks real fancy, Kettleman. I'll give you forty grand for the lot like I promised. Put it back in the bag. I'll have to go out for money."

Kettleman sniffed. "I don't like that, Stickpin Brady. You always had the money here."

Stickpin smiled thinly, "After the way you got the best of me last time, Kettleman, I've learned to be cagey. You're the first man to get the best of me."

Stickpin noticed Kettleman swell a little with pride at this statement. He went on, "I've got the money in the all night bank on Bridge Street. You can stay here with the junk until we get back. We'll have a drink on it before I leave."

Carelessly, Stickpin walked to the liquor on the table. His back was toward Kettleman and Gates. He drew his long, thin hand from the pocket of his immaculate coat, and concealed in that hand was the bottle of poison. He flipped the cork out with his thumbnail, and picked up the bottle of scotch with the same hand.

Into the first glass, he poured Scotch and poison at the same time. Into the other two glasses he poured scotch only.

As he triggered soda into the whiskey, he slipped the empty poison bottle back into his pocket. Then he turned toward the table with the drinks carefully placed in his hand.

Kettleman was just scraping the last of the jewelry into the bag with his pudgy hand. Brady gave him the first drink. He gave Gates one of the other two, and kept one for himself. Raising his glass, Stickpin Brady said:

"I'm forgetting the past, Kettleman. Here's to the future. May you and I do a lot more business." He drained his glass smoothly.

Gates gulped his drink like a thirsting man. Kettleman downed only half of his drink and set the glass down. A gleam of satisfaction flickered in Stickpin's beady eyes. There had been enough poison in that drink to kill three men. Within half an hour, Kettleman would discover the truth, and it would be too late.

Stickpin went to the closet for his coat and hat. He returned with the black bag he had planted there. He stopped just behind Kettleman's chair and put his bag down. Kettleman was staring at his empty glass. He had finished his drink!

Stickpin addressed Gates. "Come on, Gates," he snapped. "We'll make a fast trip to the bank and be back inside half an hour."

Kettleman grunted. "I'll be right here, buddy," he snarled.

Stickpin thought to himself, "You're damned right you will!" He reached down swiftly, and picked up the bag with the real jewels in it, leaving the one with the paste imitations. He felt sure that if Kettleman should glance into the bag to reassure himself, the glass, in the dim light, would allay his suspicions.

Then he and Gates were out in the hall—going down in the elevator— walking casually out into the almost deserted street. Gates was chuckling.

"You seem to be enjoying this business," Brady snapped.

"Slick job," Gates rumbled. "What's goin' to happen when your pal gets tired of waiting?"

"He won't get tired," Stickpin snapped with veiled meaning. "You get in and drive that car like hell out to the airport. We've got to clear the border before morning. That ice is worth eighty grand if it's peddled right."

GATES chuckled again, slipped the car into gear and slid out into the traffic.

Ten minutes later, a low-wing monoplane with the twin seats side by side in the open cockpit, was biting up from the airport. Gates was gunning the Wright engine to a frenzy of roaring power. The trim ship grabbed altitude in a steep zoom. Up—up—up!

Brady was gripping the edge of the cowling with his prong-like fingers and his face seemed more green than blue. Damn his guts, they kept acting up! There wasn't anything to be afraid of. Millions of people were flying every day.

Gates looked over at Brady, and chuckled again. He could tell by Brady's fixed expression just what fears were drumming through his mind.

"Stop that infernal laughing!" Brady rasped out.

"Sure, boss, sure. Scared, ain't you?"

"No—no, I'm not scared. Head south until you cross the mountains, and keep off the airways."

Gates shot a glance at the black bag that Brady was clinging to with one hand. Brady was trying to look over the side. The yawning black void below seemed to be waiting—waiting to suck him down. He laughed nervously, for no reason. Hell, Gates was a good flyer. He had come well recommended. Millions of people were flying. . . .

The ship gave a sudden lurch. Brady wilted. The bottom seemed to fall out of his stomach. Bracing his feet against the floor, he jerked a look across at the pilot. Then he choked.

Gates was writhing in his seat like a worm on a hot stove. His eyes were protruding from his head and his tongue lolled from his gasping mouth. His hand seemed to have no control over the teetering stick between his knees.

"For God's sake, man, what's the matter!" Brady managed to scream above the roar of the engine. A dull, throbbing fear was beating through his blood.

"I'm burnin'—burnin' up," Gates husked through the froth on his lips. "The pain—pain. . . ."

Realization like a club hammered at Brady's horrified brain. He dropped the bag in that grim moment. Put his hands to Gates' shoulders and tried to hold him in the seat.

"Gates—Gates," Brady husked, fear of death in his voice, "what liquor did you drink back there?"

Gates was screaming now, tearing at his stomach. His face was twisted into a horrible mask of torture. Through stiffening jaws he coughed out the words:

"I—I finished Kettleman's—drink— he didn't want. . . ."

Gates was stiffening in the seat, his hand frozen to the stick. The ship was lopping over in a crazy spin. Brady stared out into the blackness. The icy wind against his face was death breathing upon him. As the ship hurtled toward the earth, the roaring engine seemed to scream:

"Poison enough to kill three men— three men—three men. . . ."

The End

SHORT CIRCUIT TO HELL
By MAURICE GIMBEL

*Any murderer can get electrocuted by the state, but it takes a clever
lad like Slick Nash to figure a way to save the law the expense!*

The roar of Nash's weapon caromed from the walls

"SLICK" NASH, taking a small-
town vacation from a bank
stickup that misfired, sat back
on the hotel veranda and appeared
asleep while he listened to the com-
ments of Sheriff Ben Tupper. The officer was talking about a prosperous looking farmer who had just come out of
the one-story bank building across the
street and had driven off in an old model
roadster.

Watching the dust of the car receding
in the distance, lounging with his back
to Nash, the sheriff said to the towns-
man who was helping him rest: "Looks
like Bart Fanning's gittin' might skittish about his money these days.
Reckon that's what comes when a man
gets to makin' more'n he's used to."

"Feller's got a right to be skittish
about the bank," commented his hearer.
"That old brick vault wouldn't be safe
against a man with a good sized fire-
cracker, much less these modern safe
breakers. Old Fanning's wise to move
his money to the city where it'll be
safer."

"Still, I wouldn't feel any too good
takin' that pile o' his out an' nursing
it in a place as isolated as that farm o'
his. A man could rob him and nobody'd
know it for a week. I was out lookin'

108

over that modern electrical machinery he's just bought the other day, and I tell you, his place is as remote and spooky as a haunted house. And he lives there alone, sleeping in that old house nights—not me."

Nash, cupping a light to a cigarette, outwardly a casual listener, felt the quickened beat of his pulse at the thought of what this knowlegde could mean to him. This was almost as good as finding a bag of gold.

He watched the disappearing dust whirl with a steady, motionless regard. He was suddenly sure that Bart Fanning would be having an unexpected guest. . . .

LIGHTNING spread a momentary pale web above the hills when Nash hid his coupe in a covert of dense bushes just off the rutted back road near Bart Fanning's farmhouse.

Vaulting the rail fence Nash knelt beside a haystack and set a match to a twisted piece of newspaper soaked with gasoline from the coupe's carburetor.

The flame leaped up the stack and sent a red glow waving across his face. He hesitated a moment then whirled and darted to the roadside where, crouching behind a thick-boled tree, he waited tensely.

He could still see that black satchel in his mind's eye. It hadn't looked like any penny ante business to him. It made him think of the satchel chained to the wrist of the paymaster in the attempted Pemberton Tire Company robbery. If that job hadn't gone screwy Nash would have had no need for the Carneyville hideout.

He watched Bart Fanning come across the field at a rapid, hobbling run. By the farmer's side bounded his huge Airedale watchdog. For a moment Nash watched the gaunt figure flailing at the flames with a wet burlap sack.

Then stealthily he crept from behind the tree. The latch on the rear door of the farmhouse hadn't caught. Nash chuckled and went into the large, barely furnished living room. Bart would be busy with the fire for quite a while— alone. After six o'clock on a Saturday night, Nash knew, all the farmhands were in town to make a night of it.

Nash examined the room. Where did the old goat cache his dough? In a corner of the room leaning against the wall stood a double barreled shotgun. Nash smiled at it thinking of how some of the other monkeys from the big town might have messed up this set-up by being too cocky. But not Nash. No he was playing it safe and easy; you could trump these appleknockers any other way, but they were aces with a shotgun. He emptied the weapon.

He searched an ancient roll-top desk. No soap! Then he lifted the lid of a high, round-topped trunk.

There it was! The black bag was in the trunk.

Hunkered down on his heels Nash whistled softly against his teeth as he inspected the contents of the satchel. Not all of it was negotiable—there were some stock certificates—but plenty was: long-green thousands! He could hop down to Mexico; there would be dice games, dangerous eyed senoritas with ivory skins, plenty of tequilla—

Rain spitting against the window finally aroused him. Geez! How long had he been squatting there half hypnotized?

What was that?

He spun around, warned by the creaking complaint of the seamed floor. One flash he got of Bart Fanning's soot-blackened face. He sent his hand streaking under his armpit.

"Git 'im boy!" Fanning roared. The Airedale launched himself in a snarling leap. Bart plunged for his shotgun.

The roar of the explosion of Nash's weapon caromed from the walls as

Nash snapped a shot at Bart's plunging form. The dog's teeth burned across the flesh of his hand and ripped his glove to shreds.

Bart lurched; his horny palm slapped against the shotgun's stock. Then he pitched forward on his face with blood welling from behind his left ear.

NASH clubbed his gun and whacked viciously at the dog's head. At last, struggling for breath, he straddled over it where it lay stretched upon the floor, stained with bright red.

"Satisfied, are you," Nash panted. There was no sound in the room except the ticking of the clock but he could hardly hear it for the wild drumming of his heart.

A note fallen from Bart's pocket caught his eye. Unfolded the words "will be over to see you about *eight-thirty* Saturday night, dad" leaped out at him.

His eyes flicked to the clock on the mantel.

Eight fifteen!

Within fifteen minutes Bart's son would be here!

He had to think quick—had to make things look normal so that Bart's son would sit around for an hour or so not thinking anything was wrong while he, Nash, Mexico-bound, made a getaway.

He dragged Bart's heavy body to the closet and hid it there. He placed the dog's body beside him. Breathing quickly he straightened the room and wiped away all trace of the crime. It was twenty after eight.

What else had to be done? O.K., all set—no wait, dammit—one little slip could land him in the electric chair. The phone wire! The son could telephone and spread the alarm hours sooner. He decided to cut the wire outside the house—too noticeable if it were cut inside.

The rain had stopped when Nash splashed across the sodden mire of the yard to the garage. He searched with clumsy haste in the darkness. He finally found a ladder and, swearing, as it bumped and rattled against the new machinery stored there, he dragged it out.

Nash propped it against the side of the house, located the wire running by the wall, and with a pair of heavy pliers taken from hi scar cut into it. Mexico.

At nine thirty the telephone in Sheriff Ben Tupper's office rang.

"H'lo," Tupper drawled; "who's callin'?"

It was Ed Fanning, the farmer's son. As the sheriff listened to the almost incoherent message coming across the wire Ben Tupper's indolence vanished.

"What? Bart dead? Hold everything Ed—I'm on my way."

A half hour later the sheriff drove his ramshackle flivver up the lane to Fanning's place. Ed Fanning—his face a pallid mask — stumbled out of the farmhouse and stood quivering in the beam from the headlamps.

Brokenly Ed told about how he had waited in the house for Bart, thinking he was out but would be back soon. How finally he had noticed a curl of blood seeping from the closet—and then the horror of his discovery when he had looked inside.

"See anybody loafin' around? Searched the grounds yet? Lot o' mud tracked in; did you try to follow the tracks?"

"No," answered the youth. "I was too plumb upset."

"TIME'S what counts," the sheriff said with a new tone that entirely belied his usual indolent attitude. "Every minute gives the killer that much more distance. Always ought to look for him before you do anything else. Le's look around. Got a flashlight?"

That was how they came to the side of the house, and saw the ladder leaning against it. Then the sheriff's foot came into contact with something yielding, and he shot the yellow cone on the ground at the foot of the ladder.

There, in the mud, was a body.

The sheriff turned the light on the dead face half buried in the mud. "Seen this feller before, at the hotel at Carneyville—think his name's Nash."

He knelt down and put his hand on Nash's chest but there was no heartbeat. His slow eyes shifted from the face of the dead man, and he cast the beam of light upward. He saw the electric wire running under the eaves of the house.

Then the sheriff picked up the pliers beside the murderer's body. As the youth stood beside him, the sheriff's voice came in a grunt.

"You see what that dirty critter done, son?" he asked kindly. "He aimed to cut the phone wire but instead cut into that new high-tension power wire yore dad run in for his power tools. Murder calls for electrocution in this state, son—an' this gent didn't lose no time executin' his own sentence."

The End

Satan Is a Hitch-Hiker
(Continued from Page 81)

thought I was seeing a ghost. For, as sure as my name is Oscar Morgan, when I bore down on that automobile the dead man in it suddenly jumped up and looked me straight in the eye.

"The next moment the car shot forward and began racing down the highway hell bent for election. But I kept right on behind it. If I do say it myself, I'm a hell of a good driver and that punk in the other car wasn't so hot. Pretty soon I was racing hub to hub with that ghost or whoever he was. I

(Please Turn Page)

Satan Is a Hitch-Hiker

followed the trail for three miles. Then I came abreast of the other car, cut in front of that man—or ghost—or whatever it was, and forced the driver toward an embankment.

"There was not a thing on God's earth he could do them, but crash head on or stop. So he stopped. I jammed on my brakes, jumped out of my car and got out my gun, ready to shoot.

"Then all hell seemed to break loose. The man in the other car struck first. The bullet hit me in the left arm. I knew he was aiming at my heart and that he meant to kill me like a dog.

"I thought to myself, 'I must be calm.' I shot straight through the windshield of the car and hit the man right between the eyes.

"Then I searched him and found papers that identified him.

"HE was as I had thought, not ghost but fiend! He was the hitch-hiking murderer, Chester Comer, and he was dying from the wound that I had inflicted. They said so at the hospital.

" 'Did you kill Simpson?' they asked.

" 'Yes,' said the dying murderer.

" 'What about Ray Evans?'

" 'I killed him too,' he mumbled. He was so far gone by that time you could almost hear the death rattle.

" 'Come on, come on,' a frantic detective urged him, 'tell us where you hid the bodies. Don't you understand? You're dying.'

"Comer gasped for breath. His eyes were glassy. 'Pipe line,' he said feebly.

"As the officers leaned forward to catch his last words they called off the names of others who were missing.

" 'What about them?' they demanded, 'did you kill them and hide their bodies?'

" 'Oh, piles of bodies,' Comer gasped. And those were his last words!"

MANY WOMEN TESTIFY TO ITS
RELIEF FOR DELAY
DELAY DOESN'T BOTHER ME NOW SINCE I WAS TOLD ABOUT PERIO RELIEF COMPOUND

331978